"I had some government visitors who warned me about you," Kendall said.

"And yet you continued to see me." Alexei gazed into her gray eyes. "Why?"

"Because they were wrong."

"And how did you know that?"

She knew without reservation that what she felt for this man, whether he ever returned her love or not, was something that would always be with her. "Because I love you," she said softly, "and I could never love a man who was less than honorable."

Alexei's heart sank at her words. "Oh, Kendall, do you have any idea what you're saying? You realize, don't you, that there can't be any kind of relationship between us?"

"I don't agree with that at all. I'm telling you what I feel, what I've felt ever since I met you."

Alexei sighed as he rested his forehead against hers and looked into her eyes. "I knew you were going to be trouble the minute I saw you."

Dear Reader,

Welcome to Silhouette—experience the magic of the wonderful world where two people fall in love. Meet heroines that will make you cheer for their happiness, and heroes (be they the boy next door or a handsome, mysterious stranger) who will win your heart. Silhouette Romance reflects the magic of love—sweeping you away with books that will make you laugh and cry, heartwarming, poignant stories that will move you time and time again.

In the coming months we're publishing romances by many of your all-time favorites, such as Diana Palmer, Brittany Young, Sondra Stanford and Annette Broadrick. Your response to these authors and our other Silhouette Romance authors has served as a touchstone for us, and we're pleased to bring you more books with Silhouette's distinctive medley of charm, wit and—above all—*romance*.

I hope you enjoy this book and the many stories to come. Experience the magic!

Sincerely,

Tara Hughes
Senior Editor
Silhouette Books

BRITTANY YOUNG

The White Rose

Published by Silhouette Books New York

America's Publisher of Contemporary Romance

SILHOUETTE BOOKS
300 E. 42nd St., New York, N.Y. 10017

ISBN: 0-373-08640-7

First Silhouette Books printing April 1989

Printed in the U.S.A.

Books by Brittany Young

Silhouette Romance

Arranged Marriage #165
A Separate Happiness #297
No Special Consideration #308
The Karas Cup #336
An Honorable Man #357
A Deeper Meaning #375
No Ordinary Man #388
To Catch a Thief #424
Gallagher's Lady #454
All or Nothing #484
Far from Over #537
A Matter of Honor #550
Worth the Risk #574
The Kiss of a Stranger #597
A Man Called Travers #622
The White Rose #640

BRITTANY YOUNG

lives and writes in Racine, Wisconsin. She has traveled to most of the countries that serve as the settings for her Romances and finds the research into the language, customs, history and literature of these countries among the most demanding and rewarding aspects of her writing.

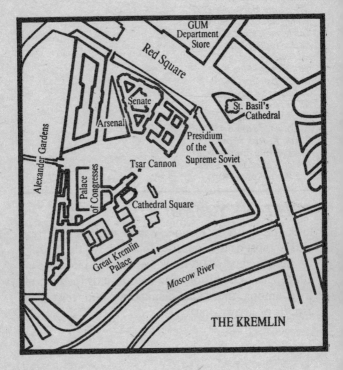

Prologue

Alexei Demyenov sat behind his desk at the Soviet embassy in Washington, D.C. and studied the KGB agent seated across from him with a quiet intensity most would have found disconcerting. "I have neither the patience nor the time for your innuendo, Breskov," he said in Russian. "Try being direct for a change and tell me what it is that you want."

"I thought I'd made myself clear, but apparently I was mistaken." He tossed a letter onto the desk in front of Alexei. "This is from a woman named Kendall Stuart."

"And her business is?"

"Arranging for information-sharing between the academics of this country and others."

Alexei read the letter and shrugged. "What has this to do with me?"

"She wants to arrange a conference in Moscow."

"I gathered that from the letter."

"We're going to let her."

"All right. But I repeat, what has this to do with me?"

"I want you to be the one who meets with her and starts the negotiating process."

"That's hardly in my area of expertise," Alexei said.

"Then you will soon be making it your area of expertise. I want you to get as close to her as you can."

"Why?"

"Because of who her father is."

Alexei waited impatiently for the man to continue. "Must I prompt you all the way through this conversation or can you make it from one point to the next on your own?"

The young agent's eyes narrowed. He neither liked nor trusted Alexei Demyenov and made no secret of that fact. "Her father is Gen. Craig Stuart, the man in charge of U.S. strategic defense operations in Europe."

"Ah," Alexei said as he leaned back in his chair. "And you want me to find out what his daughter knows."

"Exactly. You must make her fall in love with you. You must make her want to confide in you. Her father dropped out of sight. We think he's in Europe, but his movements are so well protected that none of our sources know for sure. Something is going on and we need to know what."

Alexei pushed the letter back across the desk. His brown eyes were alight with amusement.

Boris Breskov didn't like being laughed at. "You find something funny, comrade?"

"I do. You would, as well, if you'd stop your inept scheming and plotting long enough to think about it. Do you honestly suppose that this man, who holds his country's safety in the palm of his hand, brings home a map at the end of a hard day at the Pentagon and says to his wife and daughter, 'We decided to deploy missiles here, here and here?'"

"Of course not."

"Then what do you imagine this poor girl knows?"

"That's what I expect you to find out." He got to his feet, and without saying anything else, he strode rigidly from the room, nearly running over the Soviet ambassador who had just started through the door.

At the sight of the elderly statesman, Alexei rose from his chair with a warm smile. "Fyodor. How are you today?"

"Fine, fine. What has young Boris in such a rage?"

"He feels that I don't take him seriously enough."

The ambassador eyed Alexei as he sat in a comfortable chair across from him. "That would be a mistake on your part. He may be young, but don't underestimate either his power or his ambition. Don't make an enemy of him."

"I'm afraid it's too late for your warning." Alexei resumed his seat.

The ambassador studied Alexei with intelligent blue eyes in a face that had once been handsome but was now lined by time and worry. Alexei had become like a son to him during their years together in America. The younger man, through his openness and his ability to articulate his country's policies, had single-handedly done more to create good will between the American press and the Soviet government than anyone had achieved before him. It had made him a highly visible and popular figure both in the States and in Russia. But it had also made him some powerful enemies, and Fyodor Brodsky feared for him. "I suggest you pacify the man as much as you can without selling your soul."

"I don't think it can be done. For the purpose of collecting information, he wants me to see a woman who undoubtedly knows nothing."

The ambassador shrugged. "Then see her a few times, tell him you found out nothing and that will be an end to it. Nobody loses, everybody wins—including the girl. Who knows what kind of man he'll aim at her if you refuse?" He got to his feet. "And now, I have an appointment. We'll talk later."

Alexei watched the ambassador leave, then dragged his fingers tiredly through dark hair that was just starting to go prematurely gray at the temples. He hated this necessity to play games.

Picking up the letter the agent had left behind, he stared at it for a long time, then reached for his phone. A buzzer sounded at his secretary's desk in the outer office. "Please get me a Miss Kendall Stuart," he said when she answered.

Chapter One

Kendall Stuart looked at her watch for the fifth time in as many minutes. "Excuse me," she said politely, as she leaned forward toward the driver of the taxi, "but I'm already late for my appointment. Can't you go any faster?"

Bloodshot eyes looked at her reflection in the rearview mirror. "Lady, you want to drive, get a car."

Kendall sat back in her seat and pushed her shoulder-length, honey-colored hair behind her ears. She had a car, but she'd left it at the office just to avoid having to maneuver in this traffic.

She let another minute pass before again looking at her watch—just as the taxi came to a grinding halt in the middle of the noon-hour Washington, D.C. traffic. "Oh, no," she said in quiet distress.

The driver glanced at her again in the rearview mirror and this time took pity on her. "Hey," he said with gruff kindness, "I've been in this spot before. The restaurant you want is only four blocks from here. If I were you, I'd hoof it the rest of the way. It'll be a lot faster than this."

Kendall was desperate. Glancing at the meter to see what she owed, she reached into her purse and handed the money to the driver over the back seat. "Four blocks straight down?"

"Two down, two north. It's on the right hand side of the street. The entrance is under a yellow canopy."

She flashed him a grateful smile. "Thanks." Climbing out of the cab, she carefully picked her way through the stalled traffic to the sidewalk, then walked as quickly as her high heels would allow. As soon as she turned the corner, the restaurant's canary yellow canopy flashed at her like a friendly beacon in the summer sun and she walked even faster, slowing only to pass through the revolving door. Striding through the foyer and into the restaurant itself, she found herself behind several groups of men waiting to be seated. It seemed a lifetime before the captain finally approached her with a polite smile. "May I help you?"

"My name is Kendall Stuart. I'm supposed to meet a Mr. Alexei Demyenov."

"Ah, yes, Miss Stuart. He's waiting for you." The man imperiously snapped his fingers and a white-jacketed waiter appeared. "Take this lady to Mr. Demyenov's table."

He inclined his head. "Of course. Follow me, please."

She did, keeping her eyes glued to his back as they threaded their way through the crowded restaurant. He stopped finally at a table near a window, and Kendall found herself looking up into a pair of velvet-brown eyes. She automatically extended her hand. "Mr. Demyenov, I'm Kendall Stuart."

He took her hand in his and held it. "Ms. Stuart."

Kendall sat in the chair the waiter held out for her directly across from the Soviet and watched as he resumed his own seat in front of some papers he'd spread out on the table.

"I'm sorry I'm late. I should have made a time allowance for the noon traffic."

"That's all right. It's the first time all day that I've had any time to myself," he told her as he put some, but not all, of the papers into his briefcase. "What would you like to drink?"

"Mineral water, please."

"Two," he said to the waiter, then turned his attention to the woman across from him. She had the loveliest pair of eyes he'd ever seen—a clear soft gray with thick dark lashes. "The reason I asked you here is because I understand from my government that you're interested in bringing a group of Americans into the Soviet Union to share information and ideas with Soviets of the same educational caliber." His tone was crisp and businesslike.

Kendall took the elaborately folded napkin from her plate and spread it over her lap. This was an important interview, and even though she was nervous she was determined not to look it. "That's right. I've arranged similar events between the United States and other countries and they've met with a great deal of success. Just a few months ago, for instance, I took a group of American doctors to Africa."

"I know. I've done some checking into both you and your corporation." He turned some of the pages and Kendall watched as his eyes scanned the Cyrillic lettering. "I see that you started arranging these exchanges about two years ago. What got you interested?"

She waited until the waiter set down their drinks and left, then her eyes met the dark brown ones of the man across from her. "It's complicated."

"Most worthwhile things are."

Her quick smile charmed him despite his determination not to be charmed. "True." Then she grew more serious. "When I was a child, I traveled the world with my parents. It never ceased to amaze me how much the United States was—and still is—misunderstood. Not just the government, but the people. And by the same token, I found there were many areas of the world misunderstood completely by Americans. These conferences—these times of mutual sharing of ideas and knowledge—benefit everyone involved by opening their eyes to different perspectives. Or at least by making the attempt."

Alexei's eyes roamed over her lovely face. "You're very idealistic."

Kendall looked at him curiously. "The way you said that sounds almost like an insult."

"I meant no offense. Perhaps a better word would be naive."

"Better, but no less insulting," she said, completely unoffended. "I prefer to think of myself as optimistic."

"I'm sure you do."

"And what word would you use to describe yourself, Mr. Demyenov?"

"Assuming we're speaking of political attitudes, I'd have to say that I'm cynical, though I'd venture a guess that at this moment you're thinking of me more in terms of what you Americans have so elegantly named donkeys."

Kendall had just raised her glass to her mouth and nearly choked on her mineral water.

A corner of the Soviet's mouth lifted. "Are you all right?"

She set down the glass and cleared her throat. "Yes, thank you."

"You surprise easily."

"I'm just not used to having my thoughts read so accurately."

He lifted his glass to her. "I deserved that."

Kendall studied the man across from her, and tried to gauge what he was thinking, but she'd set herself an impossible task. He was unreadable. So Kendall, being true to her nature, opted for a more direct approach. "We seem to have gotten off on the wrong foot here and I don't quite know how that happened."

"I think," he said after a moment, "that the fact that you are American and I'm Soviet is sufficient explanation."

Kendall leaned back in her chair, her eyes on his. "I thought your job was to promote good relations between the people of our countries."

"Between your press and my country."

"An interesting distinction."

"And a very definite distinction. But to get back to the matter at hand, we're interested in your proposal."

Kendall's lips parted softly in surprise. "You are?"

The grooves in his cheeks deepened attractively. "We are."

"That's wonderful!"

"And apparently unexpected," he remarked dryly.

"Well, you didn't seem very receptive. I just assumed . . ."

His eyes roamed over her face. "Never assume anything."

"Alexei!" a senator Kendall recognized called out as he approached the table. "How have you been?" Then he looked at Kendall and she saw him literally pause. "And Kendall Stuart. This is a pleasant surprise."

"Senator Martin," she said politely as she extended her hand.

He shook it and then promptly ignored her as he turned to Alexei. "Your name came up in a meeting the other day."

Alexei inclined his head toward Kendall apparently in apology as he rose to speak with the senator. Kendall didn't mind the interruption. For the first time she had a chance to really study Alexei. He was tall, perhaps six foot four, with a strong body that even the conservative dark suit he was wearing couldn't disguise. He was probably somewhere in his mid-thirties. His face was interesting with clean, straight features that were etched with character. She'd seen him on television many times patiently debating American journalists. And something she'd particularly noticed about Alexei Demyenov was that no matter how provoked he was, he never lost his temper. And yet with her he seemed different. Perhaps because the cynicism he claimed to have was more evident. He was a curious mixture of a man.

When Alexei and the senator finished their discussion, the senator looked at Kendall very closely, then he left. Alexei sat down, his eyes on her. "Are you familiar with many of the politicians in Washington?"

"A few. It's hard to work here and not be."

Alexei didn't say anything for several moments. "As you're probably already aware, as soon as we decided to consider your request, we ran a background check on you."

"I assumed that would be done."

He again glanced at the papers in front of him, quickly turning the pages. "Your father is Gen. Craig Stuart?"

"That's right."

"And he's currently with the Department of Defense?"

"I'm sure you already know the answer to that."

"I'm just trying to ascertain the facts."

"That's fine, but I really don't see what my father has to do with my request."

The waiter returned at that moment. "Are you ready to order?"

Alexei looked at her.

"I'd like a chef's salad."

"And I'll have a club sandwich."

The waiter removed the two unopened menus and left.

Alexei turned his attention back to Kendall. "Where were we?"

"I had just asked you what my father had to do with my request."

"Ah, yes. Nothing really, but you must realize that because of the sensitive nature of your father's job, we would look at your application to enter our country with a little more attention than we would give to the application of a more ordinary civilian."

"I see."

"Does your relationship with your father help you at all in setting up these conferences?"

"Is that for the record or just to satisfy your curiosity?"

"My curiosity."

Kendall studied him for a moment and then answered the question. "No. Most people never make the connection, and I don't bring up his name."

"That's probably wise. In this particular case, your father's current position is one of the strikes against you."

"I see."

"Do you?"

"I disagree, but I understand. I'd like to assure you, however, that what my father does for a living has no bearing on this conference."

He studied her for a long moment, inclined his head and and glanced down at his notes. "It says here that you live in Virginia instead of Washington."

"Yes."

"Why is that?"

Once again, Kendall failed to see the relevance, but she wanted to land that conference in Moscow. "I've always liked the country better than the city."

He gazed into her clear eyes—eyes a man could lose his soul in. Alexei looked back at his papers just so he could stop looking at her. "As you know," he continued, changing the subject completely, "before we can make any definite plans, I'll need a list of the people you propose to bring to Moscow and their educational backgrounds as well as the topics they'd like to cover."

"Of course," Kendall agreed. "I already have that information in my files, along with a tentative schedule for the conference. I'll messenger it over to your embassy this afternoon."

The waiter returned with their food and set it in front of them, then left as quietly as he had come.

"If the people meet with your approval, when would you like the conference to be held?" Kendall asked.

"Probably in December."

"All right. That gives us plenty of time." A smile suddenly curved Kendall's mouth as she took a bite of the salad.

"What are you thinking?" Alexei asked curiously.

Her smiling eyes met his. "December in Moscow. It doesn't have quite the ring of April in Paris."

He smiled also, surprising Kendall with the warmth she saw. "Nothing has quite the ring of April in Paris. But Moscow has its own charms, as you'll see."

"I'm looking forward to it. Russia has always been such a mysterious place to me."

"Mysterious?"

Kendall nodded. "Um-hm. I can remember sitting in school and staring at the map of the world my teachers kept on display over the blackboard. Other countries, like Japan, France, Brazil—they evoked colors and smells in my imagination. But Russia was different. She just sat there, huge and silent." She ate another bite of salad. "Where in the Soviet Union are you from?"

"I have a place in Moscow that I use when I'm working, but my real home is in Leningrad."

"Is that where your family lives?"

"I'm all that's left of my family."

"What happened?"

"My grandparents died in the German siege of Leningrad during World War II and my parents were killed in a train wreck when I was nine."

"You were only nine?" Kendall's compassionate heart was touched. "What did you do without any family?"

"For a year I survived by working at odd jobs, but then someone reported me and I was taken in by the state to be raised and educated."

"Oh," Kendall said softly.

Alexei lifted an expressive brow. "There's no need to look like that. It wasn't so bad. I was very well cared for."

"Maybe it's just the way you said 'the state.' It sounded so—impersonal."

"It was, but it was certainly better than being on the streets and living in abandoned buildings."

"You've come a long way since then."

"I suppose I have."

"How did you get from a state orphanage to where you are today?"

"It was a shorter road than you might think. I was always good at debate, which got me into law school. When I finished that I practiced law for a time and taught."

"And then?"

"And then I was assigned this job."

"Do you live in the United States most of the time?"

"I have for the past few years." Alexei looked at her quietly. He couldn't remember the last time he'd talked so much about himself and it made him uncomfortable. "Have you almost finished with your lunch?" he asked suddenly. "I have another appointment."

Kendall took a final bite and put down her fork. It was her own fault for being late in the first place.

Alexei inclined his head toward their waiter who came immediately with the check. He signed it, then walked around the table to Kendall and pulled her chair out for her. As they left the restaurant, she was intensely aware of his hand resting firmly in the middle of her back.

"Where's your car?" he asked as they walked outside into the bright sunlight.

"I left it in Georgetown and took a taxi here."

"I'll have my driver drop you off." Just as he said it, a silver Mercedes pulled up to the curb. The driver, a young man dressed in a gray suit, leaned across the front seat to the passenger side and spoke to Alexei in Russian through the open window. Alexei looked at his watch and nodded, then opened the rear door for Kendall. "Sergei will drop you wherever you'd like."

Kendall turned suddenly, not expecting the Russian to be as close as he was, and found her face within inches of his. She inhaled sharply and stepped back, but as she did so, her foot slipped from the curb. Alexei reached out and caught her before she could lose her balance, pulling her solidly and safely against his body. She stood there for a full five seconds looking into his eyes, her breathing rapid. What was wrong with her? Once again she stepped back, this time more cautiously. Her body felt warm where it had touched his. "That's really not necessary. You need your car."

"The appointment's nearby. I can walk." Alexei helped her into the car and closed the door, then signaled something to the driver and Kendall's window slid down. Alexei leaned over slightly as he looked at her. "Get that information to me and I'll get back to you as quickly as I can on whether or not you may have your conference."

"Thank you."

His eyes rested on her lovely face for a long moment. Then he straightened away from her and tapped his hand twice on the car roof. The driver immediately pulled into the flow of traffic.

Alexei's enigmatic dark eyes followed her out of sight.

"Where would you like to go," the driver asked in heavily accented English.

Leaning back in her seat, still uncomfortably aware of what had just passed, Kendall gave him the address of her Georgetown office and made a conscious effort to relax. Her gaze rested on the back of the driver's blond head. "I'm Kendall Stuart," she introduced herself.

He said nothing.

"And you are?" she coaxed.

"Sergei," he said with obvious reluctance. "Sergei Grinkov."

"Do you work for the Soviet embassy in general or Mr. Demyenov in particular?"

He looked at her reflection in the rearview mirror. "My job at the moment is to return you to your office, not to answer your questions."

"I apologize. It wasn't my intention to offend you."

Her apology was greeted with silence from the front seat.

She let it bother her for only a moment, and then her mind was off and running. If the Soviets were serious about this conference, she had a lot of work to do. A lot of preparation. She started mentally making lists.

She was still making lists when the car came to a stop in front of her brownstone office. Kendall looked around in surprise. Where had the time gone? The driver opened the door for her and she smiled her thanks, but though he looked at her intensely, he didn't return her smile. It faded. "Thank you for the ride."

He inclined his head, climbed into the car and quickly drove away.

Kendall watched curiously until he turned a corner, then lifted her shoulders in a delicate shrug and climbed the stairs to the front door. She had had the brownstone renovated into comfortable offices. The largest one was in front where her partner and a part-time secretary worked, taking up what used to be the living room, dining room and foyer. A small, fully equipped kitchen was just off that area. Up the stairs from that were two rooms, one that Kendall used for herself and another that had been set up as a conference room. Kendall walked in just as Ginny came out of the kitchen, a cup of coffee in her hand.

Ginny and Kendall were both twenty-five and had been friends since junior high school. It had been the most natural thing in the world for them to go into business together. "Well?" Ginny asked expectantly. "What happened?"

Kendall sat in an overstuffed chair across from Ginny's desk and couldn't keep her eyes from sparkling. "It looks good."

Ginny let out a little scream as she set down her coffee and sat in her chair. "That's wonderful! When will you know for sure?"

"I can't be positive, but my instincts tell me that Alexei Demyenov is a man who gets things done quickly and efficiently. I'd say in the next two weeks. A month at the latest."

"What a coup! The universities will be lining up for our help after word of this gets out."

"I hope so. Business could use a little boost. In the meantime, though, I have to get the files on all the participants copied and messengered to the Soviet embassy."

"Today?"

"Yes. The sooner, the better."

"Wouldn't you know Heather would pick today to take off?"

"She didn't know we'd need her."

"Well, that's all right. I don't have anything urgent going on right now. I can help."

"Thanks, Ginny. I really appreciate it. I'll start making the calls to the people involved to let them know what's going on." Kendall started to get up, but Ginny was looking at her so expectantly that she slowly sat back down. "What?"

"Well?"

Kendall just looked at her blankly.

"How was it?"

"How was what?"

"How was what," Ginny muttered. "Lunch, of course."

"Oh, that. It was fine."

"Fine? It was fine? Are you deliberately provoking me?" she asked, already knowing the answer.

Kendall suddenly smiled. "Oh, I see. You don't want to know how lunch was. You want to know how Alexei Demyenov was."

"Same thing. So? How was he?"

"He's—very handsome. As much so in person as he is on television."

Ginny sank dramatically back in her chair. "Be still my heart. What else?"

"He seems to be rather quiet and serious."

"Quiet and serious. That's good."

"Why is that good?"

"Because it fits his image. And is he a little mysterious?"

"If by mysterious you mean someone who disguises what he's thinking, yes, he is."

The phone rang at that moment. Ginny swore under her breath and answered it. When it became obvious to Kendall that the call was going to take a long time, she went through the phone messages and pulled out hers, then signaled to Ginny that she was going upstairs to her own office.

It was a cozy room, particularly in winter when she had a fire burning in the fireplace. It was simply decorated in pastel colors with a couch and chairs at one end, numerous plants and her white desk with oak trim near the double windows.

Kendall tossed her phone messages onto her desk for later and picked up her mail. Crossing to the other side of the room, she sank onto the couch and started reading. Or trying to read. It was difficult for her to concentrate. Her thoughts kept slipping back to lunch and Alexei Demyenov. He wasn't at all the kind of man who normally appealed to her. Too serious. And yet he disturbed her in a way she couldn't fathom. Deeply disturbed her.

"I didn't think that man was ever going to get to the point," Ginny complained as she walked into Kendall's office and sat in the chair across from her.

"Who?"

"Senator Annis. He seems to think that if he talks all around an issue, I'll eventually forget what the object of the discussion is. What a waste of time."

"Have you tried telling him that?"

"Several times. It hasn't done any good. He's a born blusterer. I really don't think I want him involved with the conference in Switzerland."

"Then don't let him go. I think it's a bad idea to include politicians in our work, anyway. Some of them are sincere, but most only want the free trip and publicity they get when the documentary comes out."

"You're absolutely right. I'll call him later, when I've managed to get my strength back." Ginny sighed as she leaned her head against the back of the chair. "How would you like to have dinner with a tired partner tonight?"

"Oh," Kendall said with genuine regret, "ordinarily I'd love to, but I have a date."

"Anyone I know?"

"Your brother."

"Where's Joe taking you?"

"There's some kind of dinner at the French embassy."

"Oh, yes. He told me about that." She frowned suddenly as something occurred to her. "I thought he was taking that Barbara Chambers person."

"He was, but she backed out this morning, so he asked me to fill in."

"Talk about being taken for granted!"

"Not at all. He'd do the same for me."

"That's true, I suppose." She shook her head. "For years I had hopes that the two of you were going to get together, but you ended up more like brother and sister than he and I are."

Kendall smiled. "I know. I like it that way."

"So does he, apparently." She reluctantly got up. "Well, back to work. Where are those conference files?"

"Upper left-hand corner of my desk."

Ginny found the pile and took half of them, then started for the door, but stopped suddenly. "So, he's mysterious, is he?" she asked, referring to Alexei.

"Very."

Ginny sighed and went down the steps.

When she'd gone, Kendall picked up the letter she'd been reading and started over. It wasn't until she was halfway down the page that she realized she hadn't comprehended a word. Rather than trying again, she put the letter down and leaned her head back against the couch, her eyes open and staring at nothing in particular.

She was looking at what was in her mind's eye: Alexei Demyenov.

Chapter Two

As soon as Kendall finished her work, she drove home. She loved going home. There was something so sane and peaceful about the sixty acres of land she now called her own. Getting out of her car, she opened the heavy iron gate, drove through the opening and then closed the gate behind her. Her three elkhounds recognized the sound of her car and came racing toward her, running alongside the car as she drove toward the small but functional stable and parked outside.

As she climbed out, the three dogs, their tails wagging madly, barked and bumped against her, each wanting her fair share of attention. Kendall hunkered down and hugged all of them, laughing as they tried to lick her face. Taking two apples from a bucket near her car, Kendall and her escorts walked outside into the sunshine to the white-fenced pasture where her horses were grazing somewhere out of sight. "Jasmine! Rocky!" she called as she gracefully climbed onto the fence to sit and wait.

The dogs were used to this routine and ducked under the fence to join the horses who came into sight within seconds. They were beautiful creatures, tall and sleek, one a dappled white, the other chestnut. They raced full out toward her, manes and tails flying, as the three dogs tried to keep up. They stopped right in front of Kendall and took the apples from her outstretched palms, chewing patiently while she rubbed their silky noses. "I don't have time tonight, but tomorrow we'll go for a long ride."

The white horse, Jasmine, moved closer, nuzzling Kendall on the side of the neck. Kendall put her arm around her and rested her cheek against the mane. She'd owned Jasmine for eight years; had raised her from when she was a colt and Kendall had been living with her parents at the time.

Kendall caught sight of her watch and clicked her tongue. "I'm going to be late if I don't get moving." With a final pat for each of the horses, she jumped down from the fence and walked along the cobblestone path to her house. It had once been a farmhouse, and still looked much as it had nearly one hundred years ago with a long porch that ran the length of two sides of the white wood house. A small table and set of chairs were at the apex where she liked to eat on nice days, and a bench swing hung at one end of the front. Clay pots of bright flowers were strategically placed. Kendall unlocked the front door and walked in, leaving the dogs to lie down on the porch. She left the second heavy door open so that the fresh evening breeze could come in through the screen door.

Previous owners had taken the formerly cramped rooms and opened them up by knocking out walls and building a central fireplace that could be enjoyed from the living room, library and kitchen. Five bedrooms upstairs had been turned into two bedrooms and an enormous bathroom/dressing room.

Kendall went to the comfortable kitchen and poured herself a glass of wine, then took it upstairs with her while she examined the contents of her closet for something to wear that night. Tending to avoid formal functions, she didn't have a lot to choose from, but she finally decided on a beautiful peacock blue taffeta that left her shoulders bare and was fitted to slightly beneath her hips, flaring out to just below her knees. It was three years old, but she seriously doubted that anyone would notice.

After a quick shower, she slipped on the dress and went to work on her face. Using makeup sparingly, she enhanced her already lovely eyes and added a pale rose pink to her lips. Then she brushed her silky hair away from her face, twisted it into an elegant knot low at the base of her neck and fastened it in place with a rhinestone-studded comb. It was an old-fashioned hairdo, but was well suited to her features and showed the delicate line of her throat.

Looking at the clock on her bedside table, she saw that it was nearly eight. Joe was always on time. She went downstairs to call the dogs into the house and took them back to a room behind the kitchen where she kept them when there were guests. No sooner had she shut them in than the front doorbell rang. "Coming!" She walked into the front hall and smiled as she opened the screen door for the handsome blond man standing there. "Hi, Joe. I'm almost ready."

He leaned over and kissed her cheek. "You look great."

She eyed his tuxedo. "So do you."

"Where are the dogs?"

"In the room off the kitchen. Why don't you say hi to them while I finish up," she said over her shoulder as she climbed back up the steps.

"Don't be too long. I don't want to be late."

Kendall took a silver clutch purse out of her closet and quickly put in a brush and lipstick, then tucked it under her arm and went back downstairs. Joe walked back into the foyer just as Kendall came down the steps. "Ready?"

"Ready."

The two of them walked out to the car. Joe opened the door for her, then walked around and climbed into the driver's seat.

"Ginny tells me you might get this Soviet conference you've been working so hard on," he said conversationally as he headed down the drive.

"I'm keeping my fingers crossed."

Joe hadn't closed the gate behind him on his way in, so now he simply drove through, got out, closed it and climbed back into the car. "Ginny's really excited," he said as he put the car into gear. "She thinks that this could be just what your firm needs for that final leap into credibility."

"She's right. This would be quite a reference for us." The two of them fell into a comfortable silence, the way good friends sometimes did without feeling awkward.

After a while, Joe glanced at Kendall. "I was just thinking about a patient. What are you preoccupied with?"

"A man," she said quietly without turning her gaze from the window.

"Any man in particular?"

"Very particular. His name is Alexei Demyenov. I had lunch with him today."

"I've heard of him."

"I think everyone has."

"The Soviets couldn't have picked a better public spokesman."

Kendall nodded. "I've watched him on television. He's very different in person."

"Different bad or different good?"

"Just different."

"Different. Okay. So tell me, Kendall, lunch was this afternoon. Why are you still thinking about him?"

"I don't know," she told him honestly. "I haven't been able to get him out of my mind all day."

Joe glanced at her profile again. He'd known Kendall for as long as his sister had, and if there was one thing that stood out about her personality, it was that she always knew where she was going and how she was going to get there. This was the first time he'd heard her sound confused. He found it—interesting.

Without saying anything else, he turned his eyes back to the road and drove the rest of the way to the embassy in silence.

Washington at night was a sight to behold with its spotlighted monuments and wide boulevards. Limousines were everywhere and, by the same token, there were very few people on the streets. It wasn't as safe as it had once been to walk in the enclosing darkness.

When they got to the lovely embassy, lights blazed in and around the building. Joe pulled in behind several cars and waited while elegantly dressed men and women emerged from the vehicles and walked inside. As soon as they'd stopped directly in front of the embassy, two uniformed young men approached the car. One opened the door for Kendall and the other opened the door for Joe, then got behind the steering wheel to park the car.

Joe, his hand under her elbow, escorted her up the steps and through the door.

"How did you get invited to this, anyway?" she asked curiously.

"I performed an emergency appendectomy on the ambassador's daughter last month."

"That's one way to meet people in high places, I suppose," she said in a low voice as they approached the reception line.

The ambassador and his lovely wife seemed genuinely pleased that Joe had come. They moved on down the line, shaking hands and making polite small talk.

"Nice people," Joe said. "Very down-to-earth."

"They certainly seem so." Kendall felt strange.

"You should see their little girl."

Joe's words became indistinct to Kendall, as though he were speaking to her from a great distance. Her awareness gradually became concentrated on the fact that someone was looking at her. She could feel it. It was such a strange sensation. As though involuntarily compelled, Kendall turned her head and found her gaze drawn across the heads of dozens of people as though they didn't exist and straight to the brown eyes of Alexei Demyenov. His look seemed to burn through her.

"Kendall?" Joe said.

She didn't hear. A muscle tightened in Alexei's cheek and then relaxed.

"Kendall?"

Her lips parted softly. Alexei inclined his head slightly toward her.

A hand touched her arm and she jumped.

Joe looked at her curiously. "What's going on?"

Kendall suddenly realized that she'd forgotten to breathe. She took a deep breath, then slowly exhaled. "What?"

Shaking his head, Joe took her arm and led her toward a waiter carrying drinks. "Here," he said as he handed her one. "You look like you could use this."

She accepted it gratefully. "Thank you."

"What was that all about?"

"Alexei Demyenov's here."

"Oh, yeah?" He narrowed his eyes and searched the room. "Where? I'd like to meet him."

"I'm sure you will later."

"I guess it was lucky, at least from your stand-point, that my date cancelled. Maybe you and this Russian can get together and discuss the conference."

Kendall didn't say anything, but Joe was surprised to see that her cheeks had become delicately flushed.

"Hello, Kendall," came a deep voice from directly behind her.

Kendall stood there for a moment without moving, then took a sip of her wine. Very slowly, she turned. Alexei stood there. Their eyes met and held. "Hello."

His gaze moved slowly over her, from her bare shoulders to the hem of her dress and back again. "You look lovely."

It wasn't so much what he said as the way he looked at her when he said it that set her pulse racing. "Thank you."

Then he turned to Joe and extended his hand. "I'm Alexei Demyenov."

"Dr. Joseph Moore." Joe shook the offered hand. "Nice to meet you. I was just saying to Kendall that it was lucky she came tonight, particularly since you're here. It'll give you two a chance to talk about the con-ference."

"I see."

"And on that note," Joe continued, "if you'll both excuse me, I see someone I need to talk to."

"But Joe," Kendall said helplessly.

"I'll be back in a minute. Excuse me." And just like that, he was gone.

Kendall turned back to Alexei and for one of the few times in her life, found herself completely at a loss for words. She took another sip of wine. A big sip.

Alexei stood gazing at her and had the sudden thought that he could look upon her from now until he was a very old man and never grow bored. "Is he your—for lack of a better word—boyfriend?" he asked as he inclined his dark head toward Joe.

"No. He's just a very dear friend."

Someone approached at that moment and spoke to Alexei, giving Kendall a chance to study him. He seemed even taller in his tuxedo, his shoulders broader. He caught her look when he turned his attention back to her. "What are you thinking?"

Kendall was a little embarrassed to be caught gawking at him, but it didn't show. "That men from the Soviet Union usually disdain wearing tuxedos as being too..." she searched for the right word.

"Elitist?" Alexei suggested helpfully.

"Exactly."

"Well, mostly we try to fit in these days as best we can."

"You somehow don't strike me as being one of the crowd," she said quietly.

His eyes looked into hers. "Where I come from, being part of the crowd is exactly the thing for which we strive."

Kendall inwardly shook her head. Not him.

"Alexei," boomed a voice nearby. The man it belonged to was in his seventies, a tall man with a sure stride. "You haven't introduced me to this young lady."

She watched in surprise as Alexei smiled at the man with genuine affection. "My apologies. Ambassador

Brodsky, this is Kendall Stuart. Kendall, this is the Russian ambassador, Fyodor Brodsky."

The older man took her hand in his and lowered his mouth to it in a gallant gesture without his lips actually touching her. "I'm happy to meet you, Miss Stuart. How are you enjoying the gathering?"

"It's lovely."

"And so you answer my question without really answering it at all. You could be a diplomat." The words were spoken with quiet humor. He was a very gentle man. The kind who'd be wonderful with grandchildren. "I confess I sometimes feel that if one has been to one of these gatherings, one has been to them all. The French do a wonderful job, however. And their food—" he shook his head as he seemed to privately contemplate past feasts "—their food is always magnificent. Magnificent." He turned his smiling eyes to Kendall. "I hope to see you again, Miss Stuart." After saying something to Alexei in Russian, he wandered away, his hands folded behind his back, nodding and smiling benevolently to those who chanced to catch his eye.

"I think I like him," Kendall said, her eyes on his disappearing back.

"You sound surprised."

"Not really surprised. I just expected him to be a bit more forbidding."

"Like me?"

Kendall met his look with a direct one of her own. "You're not really forbidding," she said softly. "I think aloof would be a better word for you. At least when you're around me."

"Are you saying that I treat you differently from other people?"

Kendall countered with a question of her own. "Do you?"

Alexei looked at her for a long moment. Those gray eyes. A man could lose his soul in them. "Yes."

Dinner chimes had sounded earlier. Joe now returned and took Kendall's arm. "I think we should be seated."

Alexei inclined his head toward both of them and walked away. Joe watched him for a moment, then glanced down at Kendall and noted that she was watching him, too. "He seems like a nice enough man."

"Ummm."

"For a Soviet."

Kendall glanced at him from the corner of her eye. "You think being a Soviet makes him less nice?"

"What I think, my lovely friend, is that you'd better remember who you are and who he is and steer clear of anything but a business relationship."

"For heaven's sake, Joe. I've seen the man twice in my life."

"Look, I'm not passing judgment."

"That's nice to know."

"I'm not finished."

"Sorry."

"I'm not a particularly observant man."

"That's redundant."

"What?"

"Men in general aren't observant. It's not one of their finer qualities."

Joe smiled despite his attempt at being serious. "Guilty as charged." He grew more serious. "But even I can feel the air crackle between the two of you." He took her arm to lead her into dinner. "Watch yourself, Kendall."

There were two extraordinarily long tables, both beautifully set, each seating about forty people very comfortably. Kendall was placed next to Joe. Just as she took her seat, she looked across the table and straight into the eyes of Alexei Demyenov.

Alexei looked away first when his dinner partner spoke to him, setting her free.

Free, yet not really free. Whether she was speaking to Joe or the Frenchman seated on her other side, Kendall was constantly aware of Alexei.

The dinner was interminable. Course after course after course. Kendall took only a bite of each dish. There was no way a human being could eat the amount of food put before the guests—though Ambassador Brodsky seemed to be making some headway.

As dinner was finally finishing some three hours later and the soft strains of music floated in from the ballroom, Joe's beeper went off. He pressed the button and shook his head. "What timing. I'll be right back."

No sooner had he disappeared than a hand gently came to rest on her bare shoulder. She looked up to find Alexei there. "Dance with me."

Kendall hesitated.

"Contrary to what you apparently think, I won't bite you."

She reluctantly put her hand in his and allowed him to lead her into the ballroom. When they were out on the dance floor, Alexei turned her around. He put his hand at her waist and just looked at her for a long moment. Then he began moving rhythmically to the music, pulling Kendall closer until their bodies almost—but not quite—touched. Her senses filled with the clean smell of him. Her hand, resting lightly on his shoulder, told her that he was every bit as solid as he looked.

"Do you often come to these types of functions?" he asked, politely conversational.

"No. I'm only at this one because Joe's date had to cancel." She was so aware of his arm around her that she was having trouble concentrating on conversation.

"I take it, then, that you prefer more solitary pursuits."

"Yes."

Alexei sighed. "That's a wonderful luxury you have."

Kendall looked up at him curiously. He sounded almost sad. "Are you saying that you, too, would prefer more solitary pursuits?"

Hie eyes met hers. "Yes."

"Strange. You seem very well suited to your work."

"I am, but the public part gets tiresome at times."

"What do you like to do when you have time to yourself?"

"Read."

"What kinds of books?"

"All kinds. Why do you ask?"

"I've always thought that you can tell a lot about a person by the kinds of books he reads."

"Ah, you're trying to peer into my psyche." He grew thoughtful. "I read a lot of poetry and history. Not just Russian, but all kinds. Even American. What does that tell you about me?"

"That you're a man with broad interests."

A young man suddenly touched Alexei's shoulder. "Do you mind if I cut in?"

Alexei looked from the young man to Kendall. "As a matter of fact, I do," he said as he danced off with her.

Kendall gazed up at him, her gray eyes sparkling. "That was a shocking breach of etiquette."

"Yes, it was," he admitted without remorse.

"You're very different tonight from this afternoon."

"That was business."

"And this?"

"Is pleasure.

"Is it?"

"Do you doubt it?"

She shook her head. "I don't know what to think. You've been looking strangely at me all evening."

"I think a more accurate way of putting it would be that we've been looking strangely at each other."

"Why do you suppose that is?"

His eyes roamed over her shining hair and came to rest on her mouth. "I've discovered over the years that it's best not to dwell on some things."

Joe approached the two of them on the dance floor. "Sorry for intruding," he apologized sincerely, "but I need to talk to Kendall."

Alexei started to leave, but Joe put his hand on the Soviet's arm. He didn't want to do this, but he didn't have a choice. "I'd like to talk to you, too. There's an emergency and I have to leave. I won't be able to take Kendall home, and rather than leaving her to her own devices, I'd appreciate it if you'd give her a ride."

Kendall didn't wait for Alexei's answer. "For heaven's sake, Joe, I've been finding my own way home for years. I don't need an escort."

"I'll see that she gets home safely," Alexei said as though she hadn't spoken.

"Thanks." Joe kissed Kendall on the cheek. "I'll give you a call tomorrow."

"Joe, I . . ." Kendall began. But he was gone before she could finish. She turned to Alexei, her gray eyes flashing. "I wish he wouldn't do that."

"Do what?"

"Arrange my life for me. I meant what I said—or what I tried to say. I'll take a taxi home."

"No," Alexei said quietly, "you won't. I said I would get you home safely and I intend to keep my word."

There was something in the way he spoke that brooked no argument.

"Would you like to stay here longer or leave now?" he asked.

"If you don't mind, I'm a little tired. I think I'd like to go home."

"Then we'll go." With his arm lightly around her waist, the two of them bid their host and hostess goodbye and walked into the foyer.

Kendall saw something she hadn't noticed coming in. A round table with a vase in the middle of it filled with white roses. She walked over to them and inhaled deeply. "I love white roses," she said as she straightened.

Alexei watched her.

"Why are you looking at me like that?"

"You and white roses. If I had to choose a flower for you, it would have been a white rose. Come."

She walked outside with him.

A young man in uniform who handled parking and knew Alexei by sight ran off to get the car and returned a few minutes later.

Alexei quietly said something to the young man and handed him some money, then opened the passenger door for Kendall. He lifted the hem of her dress and tucked it in with her before closing the door and walking around to the driver's side.

The two of them were quiet as they drove. Soft strains of a Brahms piano concerto filled the background. Kendall studied Alexei's profile, shadowed in the darkness of the car, lighted with a strobe effect every so often as they passed under streetlights. Shadow, light; shadow, light. After about fifteen minutes he parked the car on a dimly lit street. "I'll be right back."

Kendall didn't ask where he was going, but relaxed back in the seat, her eyes closed, listening to the music. When he returned a minute or two later, she turned her head slightly and smiled at him.

Alexei's heart caught, despite himself. He lowered himself into the car and handed her a white rose.

She looked at it in surprise and then at him. "It's beautiful. How did you manage to find a florist open at this hour?"

"I had some help."

Kendall held it to her nose and inhaled its delicate fragrance. "Ummm. That's the nicest thing anyone's done for me in a long time. Thank you."

Alexei gazed at her for a long moment. "It gave me pleasure, Kendall."

She liked the way her name sounded when he said it.

He restarted the engine and pulled onto the street. "I know how to get to Virginia, but you'll have to direct me from there."

"All right." Again she watched him. "I noticed that you were at the embassy alone tonight."

"I usually go to those functions alone."

"So you're not seeing anyone in particular?"

"Not in the United States."

"What about the Soviet Union?"

He glanced sideways at her. "There's a woman there."

"Are you in love with her?"

"I'm thinking of marrying her."

"That doesn't answer my question."

"There is no answer to your question. I could say yes, but then my definition of the word love is probably different from yours, so my answer would, in the end, tell you nothing.''

''Turn right at the next corner.'' Kendall continued studying him. ''Perhaps it would tell me nothing and then again perhaps it would tell me everything.''

''Why are you so interested in my personal life?''

''I think because, as the evening went on and you became more of a real person to me, it occurred to me for the first time that you probably had a personal life.''

''Was I that off-putting this afternoon?''

''Yes,'' she said cheerfully. ''Turn right again.''

He did. ''I apologize. I reacted on instinct.''

''Instinct? Your instincts told you to treat me with cool disdain?''

''My instincts saw you as a threat, and they are almost never wrong about people.''

''My driveway is the next left. What do you mean that you saw me as a threat?''

''You're an American.''

''Why does that threaten you?''

He turned and stopped the car in front of the gate. His eyes met hers in the darkness. ''Because you're a very appealing American and the one thing I can't afford to do is get involved with an American woman.''

Kendall got out of the car and swung the gate open, then left it open as he drove through and picked her up on the other side.

''Why not?'' she asked as though the interruption hadn't occurred.

''Because there are too many differences, Kendall. Political and social.'' When they got to her house he parked the car, then, leaving the engine running, he walked around to open the door for her.

"Would you like to come in for a cup of coffee?" she asked.

His eyes roamed over her face, haunting in the moonlight. "It's late."

"That's true," she agreed, "but tomorrow is Saturday."

Without saying anything, he leaned his body across hers to shut off the engine. Kendall felt the contact down to her toes, and if the way he looked at her as he backed out was any indication, so did he. Alexei helped Kendall out of the car, then followed her up the steps to her house. As soon as she'd opened the front door he could hear dogs noisily barking.

"Don't mind the girls," she told him with a smile. "They're always afraid they're missing something. Come with me and I'll introduce you to them."

As he followed her into the kitchen, Alexei didn't look too pleased. "They don't sound particularly fond of strangers."

"They aren't. That's what makes them such good guard dogs. But they'll be nice to you as long as you're with me." She opened the door and let the three dogs out. They immediately took up a protective stance around their mistress, one on either side and one in front, and bared their prominent and sharp teeth at Alexei. Kendall scratched each of their heads. "Come on, girls," she said softly, "be nice. Alexei is a friend."

The snarling ceased, but they still watched him suspiciously.

"This one," Kendall said of the dog who stood directly in front of her, "is Hera. She's the mother of these two, Sniff and Jangles."

Alexei liked dogs. Hunkering down in front of them, he looked more closely. "They look like wolves."

"Yes, but they're not. They're elkhounds."

"I don't imagine you have problems with intruders on your property."

"No. I think the word is out about these three."

He stretched out his hand and let the dogs sniff so they'd get used to his scent. After a moment, Hera let him pet her, but the other two weren't ready for that yet.

"Do you really want coffee, or would you prefer tea or something like brandy?"

"Coffee." He straightened.

Kendall opened the back door and shooed the reluctant dogs outside, then filled a pot with water and set about making the coffee.

"Where are the cups?" Alexei asked, making himself at home.

"Third cabinet from the left, bottom shelf."

He went where she'd indicated and pulled out two mugs, setting them on the counter for her, then took a seat at a small round breakfast table and watched her as she moved through the kitchen in her peacock-blue dress.

"How do you like yours?" she asked, unaware of his scrutiny.

"Black."

All three dogs had their noses pressed against the screen as though they were just waiting for him to make one false move. "They're rather intimidating."

Kendall followed his gaze to the door and smiled. "It usually takes them a few hours to get used to visitors." Even as she said the words, the old-fashioned coffeepot on the stove started perking. She gave it a few minutes, then poured some of the black brew into the two mugs, handing one to Alexei. "Let's sit on the front porch," she suggested. "It's such a beautiful evening."

Alexei followed her back through the house to the bench swing. The three dogs raced around the house to the porch, lay down nearby and watched. Alexei and Kendall sat next to each other and gently swayed back and forth as they looked out into the warm night. Alexei couldn't remember the last time he'd felt such complete contentment. It was a beautiful night and out here in the country one could really appreciate it. And then there was the woman beside him. "What made you decide to live out here?" he asked.

"I've always felt hemmed in in the city, almost claustrophobic. There's no place to be alone. Out here," she said as she gazed around, "you get food for the soul and peace for the spirit." Her eyes met his. What about you? Do you have a preference?"

Alexei gazed into the distance. "I don't really know. I've never been particularly attached to any place I've lived, though I do love Leningrad."

"What about Moscow?"

He shrugged. "Moscow, while it has its sights, is a city made up mostly of bureaucrats."

"Like Washington."

A smile curved his mouth. "Like Washington. But Washington has managed to retain much of its charm. Charm isn't a word one normally associates with Moscow. Leningrad, however, is another matter. It's as light as Moscow is gray." He turned his head and met her gaze. "I'd like to show it to you." Even as he said the words, he realized how much he meant them. He loved his country and wanted to share it with her.

A movement in the pasture caught Kendall's attention. Narrowing her eyes, she saw the two horses standing there watching them. She rose and caught Alexei's hand in hers. "Come with me. I want you to meet Rocky and Jasmine."

He followed her down the steps and across the yard to the fence and watched with a half-smile as she hiked up her skirt and climbed onto the top rail to sit. Alexei stood next to her, his hand protectively at her waist to keep her from falling. "Which one is this?" he asked of the white horse who was curiously nuzzling his free hand.

"Jasmine."

"She's beautiful."

Kendall smiled like a proud mother. "And gentle."

"What about that one?" he asked of the brown horse who was intent on getting his forehead scratched.

"Rocky is like his name. Sometimes he's a doll and others he's almost unmanageable."

"Why do you keep him?"

"I can't buy and sell horses like a lot of people. They're too much like family."

The dogs ran over at that moment, barking loudly at the horses. Both animals raised their great heads and ran off. Kendall turned around on the fence and looked sternly at the three unrepentant dogs. "Shame on you, girls. You know better than that. They don't normally behave like that," she explained to Alexei. "I think they're just showing off because you're here."

"It's nice to know that I haven't lost my touch," he said dryly as he put his hands at her waist. "And on that note, I have to get going. It's late and I, for one, have work to do tomorrow."

He started to simply put her on the ground, but then his movements slowed as if he'd only just realized who he held. Kendall's hands lightly came to rest on his shoulders as he slid her body past his with a slow deliberateness that left her heart pounding. He gazed at her for a long, silent moment, his eyes roaming over her face, resting briefly on her mouth and then returning to the crystal clarity of her gray eyes. The muscle in his jaw tightened. "You're such a contradiction," he said softly. "You're so delicate, and yet you live way out here alone, and you climb fences while wearing cocktail dresses. During the day you thrive in a big, noisy city, and at night you come home to—serenity." He raised his hand to cup her cheek.

Kendall was seeing a side to this man that just hours earlier she wouldn't have guessed existed. First the rose, and now this. Beneath Alexei's sometimes-aloof exterior, there lurked a very gentle man.

Alexei moved his thumb lightly against her mouth and then his hand dropped to his side. Without saying anything, he turned and walked away from her toward his car.

Kendall could only watch as he climbed in. Unconsciously, she raised her hand to her cheek, still warm from his touch.

As Alexei put the keys into the ignition, something white on the passenger floor suddenly caught his attention. It was Kendall's rose. He picked it up and held it. He could see her standing thirty yards away. Instead of taking it to her, he held it to his nose for a moment, smelling the delicate fragrance he would forevermore associate with Kendall Stuart, then put it on the seat beside him and drove down the driveway.

Kendall watched as he drove away until his taillights were out of sight, then slowly walked back to the house, the dogs trotting behind her. She mechanically walked around her house locking doors and turning out lights.

When she got to the kitchen, she suddenly remembered her rose. She'd had it on her lap. It must have fallen off when she'd gotten out of the car. Grabbing a flashlight, she went out to where the car had been parked and looked around. No rose. She felt strangely bereft and didn't know why. After all, it was just a rose.

And yet it wasn't.

With a sigh, she went back to the house and upstairs to her room. Without turning on the light or changing out of her clothes, she lay on the bed and stared at the ceiling. Alexei Demyenov. She'd met him that morning and he'd been in her thoughts ever since.

Reaching behind her head, she picked up her pillow and hugged it tightly against herself.

When Alexei got back to his quarters at the embassy, he sat in a chair in the dark, fingering the rose, deep in thought. He reached over to pick up a book of Russian poetry by Yevgeny Yevtushenko he'd been reading the night before and slipped the rose inside it. It was unlike him to do something that sentimental. It had been unlike him to buy the rose for her in the first place. No one was more aware of his actions than he was.

Setting the book back onto the table, he crossed the room to a small bar and poured himself a drink. Someone knocked on his door and Alexei exhaled a long breath. He wasn't in the mood to talk with anyone.

They knocked again.

He took a sip of his drink. "Come."

The door opened, and in the light shining from the hallway, he saw silhouetted the last person in the world he wanted to see at the moment. "What do you want, Breskov? It's late." Alexei walked back to his chair, still without turning on any lights.

The man walked further into the room. "I saw you with General Stuart's daughter this evening."

Alexei didn't react.

"What happened?"

"I danced with her and took her home when her date had to leave. That's all."

"When are you seeing her again?"

"I don't know that I am."

"Of course you are. This conference is going to involve a lot of work."

"Work being the key word."

"You can always take the relationship a step beyond."

Alexei took a long drink, eyeing the agent over the rim of his glass. "You're not understanding what I'm telling you. It doesn't matter what kind of relationship I develop with her, she's too smart and loves her father too much to say anything, even if she knew it. Not to me or to anyone else."

"You know this after less than a day with the woman?"

"I knew this after less than an hour with her."

A smile that could easily pass for a sneer stretched the agent's mouth. "I see."

"You see nothing." Alexei put his drink on the table and got to his feet. "You've finished your business. Get out."

"You forget to whom you're speaking."

"I know precisely to whom I'm speaking. I may have to be courteous to you in public but I'm under no such constraint in private. Now either get out under your own power or I'll show you out."

"You're making a big mistake."

"I've made them before."

The clash of two strong wills was a palpable presence in the room. The man looked at Alexei long and hard, then turned on his heel and left, closing the door firmly behind him.

Alexei dragged his fingers tiredly through his hair as he walked to the window. Leaning his shoulder against the frame, his arms folded across his powerful chest, he stared outside. From here he had a perfect view of the White House, resplendent with its spotlights.

But all he saw was a pair of clear gray eyes.

Chapter Three

The next morning Kendall rose early, put on shorts and an old shirt, pulled her hair back into a ponytail and prepared to work in her garden. She and her neighbor, a retired army man who loved nothing better than to work with soil and plants, were trying to create an English country garden in her backyard. It was expensive and back-breaking, but already she could see it coming to quiet and beautiful life.

No sooner had she stepped onto the back porch, though, than the dogs, barking noisily, raced around to the front, as they did whenever she had visitors. She wasn't expecting anyone. Curious, Kendall walked around to the front and saw a car with a government license plate coming down the drive. Narrowing her eyes against the sun, she saw two men in the front seat. As soon as the car stopped, Kendall approached the driver's side. The man rolled down the window. "Miss Stuart, I'm Colonel Tate with the Department of Defense and this is Jim Kinnick with the State Department."

She looked from the driver to the passenger. "What can I do for you?"

The colonel looked down at the three dogs standing with Kendall, growling low in their throats, their teeth bared. "You might call them off so we can go inside to talk."

Kendall shushed the animals and had them lie in the shade of a tree. The two men cautiously got out of the car and followed Kendall up the steps and into the welcome coolness of her living room. They sat on the couch while Kendall sat down across from them in a comfortable chair. "Now, as I asked before, what can I do for you?"

"Miss Stuart," the colonel said, "I'm going to come straight to the point. It's been brought to our attention that you've been seeing Alexei Demyenov."

That was really the last thing she'd expected to hear. "Excuse me?"

"We had a report that you were seen socializing with a man named Alexei Demyenov."

"I wouldn't call it socializing. I met him for a business lunch yesterday and he took me home from a dinner last night when my date was called away."

The two men looked at each other and then at Kendall. "We've come here to request that you sever all ties with this man," the man from the State Department said, speaking for the first time.

"Sever all ties?" Kendall couldn't believe what she was hearing. "Since when does the government tell me whom I may or may not see, for whatever reason?"

"Believe me," Colonel Tate said as he leaned forward, "we wouldn't ask this if we didn't have good reason."

"Would you please share that good reason with me?"

"We believe that Demyenov's hooking up with you is a very deliberate maneuver."

"He's involved in some business with me."

"We know. Setting up the Soviet conference. But you will admit that's hardly his bailiwick."

That idea had actually occurred to Kendall, but she'd pushed it from her mind. "All I know is that the only word I've had so far about the conference has been through Alexei."

The two men looked at each other again as though sending silent signals.

"Will you stop that? If you have something you want to say to me, say it and then let me get back to my weekend."

The colonel nodded. "All right. I realize we have no authority to make you stop seeing Demyenov, but I want you to think about this. The Soviets have baited a big hook to catch you, and that means you have the capacity to give them something they want. Or at least they think you have. I have no idea whether or not you know where your father is and I don't want to know, but I would remind you that should word of his whereabouts leak out, important work would be severely jeopardized. Your father's very life might be put at risk.''

Kendall said nothing. She'd learned as a child how to keep a secret and that wasn't about to change now.

Both men rose. "We'll be keeping in touch with you, and we can only hope you'll do the same with us.''

Kendall stood in the doorway and thoughtfully watched them leave. Just as she was about to go back out herself, the phone rang. She went into the kitchen to answer it.

Whoever it was breathed heavily before speaking. "Kendall?''

Kendall smiled. "Hello, Ginny. For a minute I thought you were an obscene phone call. Why are you out of breath?''

"I've been running.'' She panted a few more times. "It was all I could do to press your number.''

Kendall went to the refrigerator and poured herself a glass of juice, then cradled the phone between her neck and shoulder while she lifted herself onto the counter. "I keep telling you if you'd do it more than twice a year you wouldn't have this problem. What's going on?''

"I had an interesting conversation with Joe a little while ago. He told me that Alexei Demyenov took you home from the embassy last night.''

"That's right.''

"Did he say anything about the conference?''

"Not a word.''

Ginny clicked her tongue. "Darn. I was hoping maybe they'd made a decision.''

"It's way too soon."

"I suppose."

Kendall took a long drink of her juice as she swung her legs back and forth. "I just had some interesting visitors."

"Anyone I know?"

"I doubt it. One of the men was from the Defense Department and the other was from the State Department."

"I'm impressed. What on earth did they want?"

"To warn me away from Alexei. They think he wants to pump me for information about my father."

"What do you think?"

"I can't know for sure, of course, but my instincts tell me they're wrong."

"Your instincts about people are pretty sound."

"Usually."

"Usually. As opposed to mine."

"Your instincts?"

"I don't have instincts. I have hunches. And I'm always wrong. I'll even give you an example. Remember Michael Pickles?"

"The guy you thought was a minister?"

"That's the one. And he turned out to be a male stripper."

Kendall nodded. "You're right. That wasn't one of your better hunches."

"Though he did use that little white collar in one of his acts," she said in fond remembrance, then quickly cleared her throat. "Are you doing anything exciting tonight?"

"Just reading. Maybe catching up on some letter writing. What about you?"

"Only if you consider watching *Perry Mason* reruns for the third time this week exciting."

"Some people might."

"Why don't I think I want them for my friends?"

"Frightening, isn't it?"

There was a thoughtful silence at the other end of the line. "Maybe I'll dye my hair," Ginny finally said.

"What color?"

"Brown."

"It's already brown."

"I believe in gradual change."

Kendall laughed as she slid off the counter. "You could come over to my house and spend the night. We could watch *Perry Mason* together."

"Thanks, but I don't think so. All of that fresh air makes me kind of queasy."

Kendall shook her head and smiled. "One of these days you'll come to appreciate the country."

"It'll never happen."

"We'll see. In the meantime, you have a nice weekend and I'll see you on Monday."

After she hung up, Kendall went into her backyard and followed the tree-shaded cobblestone walk through the lush green of her garden. She found the flats of flowers that Buddy, her neighbor, had brought over for her a few days earlier and set to work, going down on her knees and digging in the rich soil with a spade. When she had one of the flower beds ready, she gently lifted the small plants out of their containers one at a time, put them in the ground and packed the soil around them with her bare fingers.

It was a hot day, even in the shade where Kendall was working, and perspiration beaded her forehead and nose. Every once in a while she'd brush the back of her hand across her forehead to push the loose strands of hair away from her face, leaving a streak of dirt behind. By the time she finished the second bed, four hours had passed. She tossed the spade onto the ground next to her, sat down with her long, bare legs stretched out in front of her and leaned back on her elbows to survey what she'd accomplished.

That was what Alexei saw as he stood on the cobbled walk with Hera at his side. "You've worked hard this morning."

Kendall, startled, turned, but when she saw who it was, her quick smile flashed, charming the man. "And I'm going to pay for it with sore muscles tomorrow." She rose and brushed the dirt from the back of her shorts. Her hands were hopeless. "Sorry about the mess," she apologized, "but I wasn't expecting anyone."

"I tried to call but there wasn't an answer, and when I got hold of your partner, she assured me you'd be here."

"Is there a problem about the conference?"

"Not a problem, but as I was going over your paperwork this morning I noted some omissions that need to be taken care of before I can make my recommendations. My schedule for the next several weeks is very tight, so it was either take care of it today or put it off until next month."

"In that case, I'm glad you came. I'd like to get the answer on this conference as soon as possible so I can begin making the necessary arrangements." She looked down at Hera and smiled. "I see you've made a friend."

"Just with her. The other two were less than thrilled when I got out of my car."

"They'll get used to you." Kendall looked down at her dirt-streaked clothes. "If you don't mind waiting, I'd like to take a shower before we start."

"Of course."

"You can either stay out here or go into the house."

"Outside. It's a rare pleasure for me."

"All right. If you want anything to eat or drink, feel free to help yourself. I won't be long."

While Kendall went into the house, Alexei continued down the path. Aside from the sounds of nature, it was silent. He took off his suit coat and tossed it over the back of a white wood bench that had been placed in a shady alcove, then loosened his tie and rolled up the sleeves of his white shirt. With a tired sigh, he sank onto the bench and just enjoyed the peace and quiet.

As soon as Kendall finished her shower, she blew her hair dry and left it hanging in a silky sheet to just past her shoulders. Then she put on a loose blouse and a comfortable pale pink cotton skirt that flared out around her knees. It was too hot for stockings, so she left her tanned legs bare and strapped on a pair of low-heeled sandals.

Glancing at her watch, Kendall saw that she'd already left Alexei alone for more than half an hour, so she quickly put on some pale lipstick and went downstairs to the kitchen. After looking at her watch again, she put ice into two tall glasses, dropped in lemon wedges and filled them with tea from a pitcher in the refrigerator. With a glass in each hand, she opened the screen door with her hip. There was no sign of Alexei outside, so she followed the cobbled path into the garden and found him sitting on a bench.

He looked up as she approached, his dark eyes missing nothing. "You've put a lot of work into this place."

"I've done some of it, but I've had a lot of help from one of my neighbors," she said as she handed him one of the glasses. "I thought you might like this. It's awfully hot out here."

Kendall watched the muscles in his throat move as he tilted his head back and took a long drink.

"I have a table and some chairs on the porch, if you'd like to work outside."

"That would be fine." Alexei picked up his jacket and slung it over his shoulder on one finger as the two of them walked down the cobbled path to the house and around to the front porch. "I have to get my briefcase from the car." He handed her his tea and Kendall went on up the steps, sat down and watched while he tossed his jacket into the car, removed the briefcase and walked toward her. He was such a tall man, and so powerfully built, that it was a little startling each time she saw him.

As Alexei sat down, he moved his chair immediately next to hers. "I assume," he explained, "that you don't have your own files, so we'll have to read off of the same papers." He opened the first file, which happened to be that of a professor of political science named Harper Prescott. "You have enough information in here for almost any other country but the Soviet Union," he explained. "We like to go beyond the normal credential-type information and delve more into people's political leanings and personal lives."

"I hope I can help. I don't know all of these people personally, but I'll tell you what I can."

"What do you know about his political ideology?"

When Kendall leaned toward him to read the file, her silky hair brushed Alexei's arm and the fresh scent of her filled his senses. "I understand," she said after a moment, "that by American standards he's considered very liberal, just to the left of left. He's been active with the American Civil Liberties Union and has a history of demonstrating against American involvement in various foreign countries."

Alexei noted the information in the file, then shook his head. "Why would you select someone like that for such an important conference? I'd think you'd want people who never question anything American."

"We have some of those." She noted several names. "But the point of this whole enterprise is to have a meeting of the minds between our countries. That means involving people with diverse opinions and interests."

"You Americans are a strange breed."

"Not really. It's just that we're very secure in our freedom. Secure to the point that there's no fear that dissension is going to destroy us. Our history has shown that when we're threatened, we're very capable of pulling together as a country."

"That's true. You're a very strong people."

Kendall smiled at him, and it lit her eyes. "Why, Comrade Demyenov, you sound almost fond of us."

"It would be difficult to live here and not be." Determined to stick to business, he pulled out another file. "What about Carol Lowell?"

Kendall pulled the file slightly toward her and glanced through it. Alexei watched her. He couldn't help himself. She pushed her hair behind a small, perfectly shaped ear, exposing the soft line of her jaw and throat. Her nose was straight and just right for her face; her mouth beautifully defined with a tendency to curve upward. Her lashes were long and dark, and fanned her cheeks when she blinked. Her skin was lightly tanned and smooth, making her gray eyes even more startling than they ordinarily were.

"This particular woman," Kendall finally said, "is very interesting. She's a great believer in the Marxist system and has taught some courses along those lines."

A corner of Alexei's mouth lifted. "All right. Put me out of my misery. Why do you want her at the conference?"

"Well, for one reason, she's very, very bright and talented and I think she'll make a positive contribution. For another reason, I think it'll be a wonderful educational experience for her to see the difference between how a theory works out on paper and the somewhat less attractive reality—if you'll pardon my saying so." Kendall leaned back in her chair and looked at Alexei. "I'm hoping that if we get permission to go ahead with this, your government won't pack its conference participants with all hard-liners."

"We're somewhat less secure in our system than you are yours. I'm afraid the Soviet participants will, by and large, be very strong party people."

"What about *glasnost* and this new openness that we keep hearing about in the press?"

"Ah, yes. It sounds good, doesn't it? But the Soviet people don't really trust it yet. We had something similar when Kruschev was in power. Suddenly people were able to say what they thought, to disagree. The poets and dissidents came out of hiding and proudly signed their names to political tracts. Then one day Kruschev was gone and the new people in power changed direction yet again, bringing a curtain down on freedom of speech and arresting those who hadn't made it back underground in time."

"Are you saying that people are afraid that the same thing will happen this time?"

"Memories are long in the Soviet Union."

Kendall looked at the man next to her with new understanding. "You really love your country, don't you?"

"Nowhere in the world will you find a warmer, more generous people than in Russia. They're like innocent children, protected from the harsh realities of the world by their parental government, given only good news, not bad and yet suspecting there's something more out there than they're being told." He looked at Kendall. "I disagree frequently with the government, which is why I do what I do. It's my way of creating change from within, so that maybe the children born today will have a better world in which to grow up."

For the rest of the afternoon and into the evening, they took each American Kendall had proposed for the conference and went over personal and professional data in minute detail. Every so often, Kendall remembered what the men who'd visited her that morning had said and she'd find herself studying the man beside her. Would he do something like that? Her instincts told her no. This was a man of tremendous integrity. That was one of the things she found so attractive about him.

When they finally finished, the sun had begun to set. Alexei put the files into his briefcase and leaned back in his chair. "That was a long afternoon's work."

Kendall stretched her arms high over her head. "Mmmmm. I'm hungry," she said suddenly. "What about you?"

"I hadn't thought about it, but I suppose I am, too."

"Would you like to stay for dinner? I have a steak we could split in the refrigerator and the makings for what I'll modestly describe as a salad masterpiece."

"Modestly describe, eh?"

She grinned at him. "So what do you say?"

"I'd like that very much."

"Good. Come into the kitchen and help me with the food."

As they rose, the three dogs, who'd spent the afternoon lazing in the shade of the porch, lifted their heads but stayed where they were.

Kendall turned on lights as they walked through the house to the kitchen. She went to the refrigerator and took out the lettuce, tomatoes, mushrooms and cucumbers. "You'll find a large salad bowl in that cupboard," she said, pointing. "Knives over there and a cutting board on the counter."

"I have a suggestion," Alexei said as he got out the things. "I'll make the salad while you work on the steak."

"But what about my salad masterpiece?"

"You'll just have to settle for mine."

Again Kendall smiled. She liked Alexei when he was this way. "All right. I'll light the grill."

Feeling surprisingly at home, Alexei rinsed off the vegetables and began slicing them. When Kendall came back in for the steak, she stood behind him for a moment and peered around his arm to see how he was doing. "You've obviously done this before."

Alexei felt the warmth of her body as it lightly brushed against his own and narrowly missed his finger with the knife.

"When you live alone, you either learn to cook or eat out all of the time," he said, recovering his momentum.

"Does the woman you're seeing in Russia cook?"

Alexei turned his head slightly and looked down at her. "Do you always ask such personal questions?"

"Only when I want to know the answers."

Alexei shook his head. "Not that it's any of your business, but yes, she does. Very well."

"Don't be offended," Kendall said as she leaned forward, snitched a small slice of tomato and popped it into her mouth. "I'm just very curious about you. You're not like anyone I've ever met before." She picked up another slice of tomato and held it out for him.

Alexei's mouth brushed against her fingertips as he took it from her. Kendall wasn't ready for the shock of that contact and it showed in her eyes.

"Your salad looks delicious," she said quickly—too quickly. "I'd better put the steak on the grill." Glancing at him from the corner of her eye, she picked up the cutting board with the meat on it and went back outside. The steak hit the fire with a hiss and a sizzle, and Kendall came back in and quickly gathered up a tablecloth, napkins, plates, silverware and wineglasses. The steak was going to need turning over in a few minutes, so she rushed onto the front porch and set the table, then hurried back to the kitchen. "How's the salad coming?"

"It's finished."

"Good. Would you please get a bottle of wine out of the rack and open it? The steak will be ready in just a minute."

Alexei did as she asked. Putting the bottle under his arm, he picked up the salad bowl and headed for the porch.

When Kendall came through the front door, steak in hand, she found Alexei leaning against the railing, gazing out at the night. Without commenting, she slid half of the steak onto Alexei's plate and the other half onto hers. "Here we go."

Alexei walked around to her side of the table and held the chair out for her.

"Thank you," she said as she sat down and spread the napkin over her lap.

Alexei sat across from her, poured them each a glass of wine and raised his glass to her. "Here's to your good fortune with the conference you've worked so hard on."

Kendall raised hers as well. "Thank you. And thank you also for being so helpful."

Their eyes met and held over the rims of their glasses as they drank. Kendall dropped her gaze first, surprised by the strength of her reaction to him.

"There are your horses."

She looked up at him. "What?"

"Your horses are watching us."

Kendall turned her head and smiled. "They think they're going for a ride."

"Do you ride every night?"

"I try to. They need the exercise and I enjoy it."

"Do you alternate horses?"

"Either that, or I ride with someone."

"Would you consider riding with me?"

"You know how?" she asked in surprise.

"Believe it or not, we do have horses in the Soviet Union. And yes, I've been known to ride one now and then."

"I don't mean to seem rude, but from what you told me, I assumed you'd lived in a city all your life. When were you exposed to horses?"

"I had a lot of jobs when I was growing up. One of them was taking care of parade horses. I groomed and exercised them from the time I was twelve until I was seventeen."

"Have you ridden much since then?"

"Not at all, but it isn't something you forget."

"In that case, I'd love to ride with you—maybe after dinner." She took a bite of salad. "May I ask you a personal question?"

"Another one?" he asked dryly.

"I'm full of them."

"So it would appear."

"Does that bother you?"

His eyes met hers across the table. The only light on the porch came from the living room window. "Bother is the wrong word. I'm more used to answering questions about my government than myself."

Kendall forged ahead. "It's about that woman you're seeing back in the Soviet Union."

"Again?"

"Do I seem obsessed?"

"A little."

"I suppose I am. I just find it fascinating that you couldn't tell me whether or not you're in love with her and yet you're thinking about marriage."

"I didn't say I wasn't in love with her. I said that my definition of that word might be different from yours."

Kendall took another bite of salad. "Do you miss her when you're away from her?"

"I rarely think about her."

"Aha!"

"Aha?"

"There's my answer. You're not in love with her."

Alexei shrugged. "Perhaps you're right. But I'm comfortable with her."

"That's a horrible reason to marry someone."

"On the contrary. It's a very good reason. Those are the kinds of relationships that last."

"But you don't love her. At least not the way a man should love the woman he marries."

He seemed amused. "I see. And you, who live here alone, know all about that kind of love."

"I do and I don't. I've never felt it, but I've watched people who do."

"Perhaps not everyone is capable of that kind of emotion and has to be content with something that's— at least in your opinion—less than ideal."

"Do you really believe that?"

"All you have to do is look around you, Kendall. Washington is full of marriages based on much more practical considerations than love."

"I suppose." Her voice was tinged with sadness.

"I don't think you, however, are destined for that kind of relationship."

"Why?"

"Because you," he said softly, "tend to lead with your heart instead of your head."

"You can tell that about me after such a short time?"

"Somehow I feel as though I've known you forever."

A corner of her mouth lifted.

"What's so amusing?"

"Oh," she said between bites. "I was just thinking that I may ask personal questions, but you make personal assumptions."

"Am I wrong?"

"No, as a matter of fact. I think you're exactly right."

Kendall ate one more bite of her salad and put down her fork, then glanced at his plate. "Are you almost finished?"

Alexei shook his head as he ate the last of his steak. "You Americans always rush your meals so."

"That's because there are so many more entertaining things to do than eat."

"Such as?"

"Riding."

Alexei smiled at her. It was impossible not to. She was so full of light and life.

"Now I'm ready." He eyed her skirt as she rose. "You'll have to change, won't you?"

Kendall looked down at herself and shook her head. "Oh, no. This is fine."

Alexei arched a brow expressively, but didn't argue as they went down the steps and across to the pasture. When they got to the fence, Kendall sat on it and unstrapped her sandals. "Which horse do you want?" she asked.

"Rocky."

"He can be difficult."

"So can I."

"I'm beginning to learn that," Kendall said with a smile. "Do you need a saddle?"

"No. Come on. Let me give you a hand up." After helping Kendall onto Jasmine, he effortlessly mounted Rocky and turned the horse with nothing but the pressure of his knees.

Kendall watched him with an appreciative eye. "Well, well. I'm impressed. Are you ready to race?"

"I'm ready."

"I should warn you that I cheat."

"Cheat?"

Without any further warning, Kendall and Jasmine took off. It took Alexei and Rocky a minute to catch up, but catch up they did, and soon passed them.

Jasmine seemed to sense that her honor was at stake and ran even faster until she and Rocky were neck and neck.

"To the stream!" Kendall yelled as her skirt billowed out over the back of the horse. Both horses seemed to sense where the finish line was because with little effort on the riders' part they were soon going in that direction. Rocky was the first to splash into the knee-high water and out on the other side, but not by much. Jasmine was less than one half of a length behind.

As soon as they were on the dry embankment, Alexei jumped off his horse and walked over to Kendall. Breathless and laughing, she slid off Jasmine and into his arms.

Their laughter faded, though both of them were still breathing hard in the otherwise silent night. Alexei hesitated and then reached out and trailed the back of his fingers along the smooth skin of her cheek. "God, you're a beautiful woman, Kendall."

She raised her hand to his and their fingers twined together.

His mouth moved closer to hers. "I've wanted to make love to you from the moment I first set eyes on you."

Kendall gazed into his warm eyes and was lost.

His mouth captured hers in a slow caress that devastated her with its tenderness. As he wrapped his strong arms around her, pulling her body close to his, she raised her hands to his head and tangled her fingers in his thick, dark hair. Her mouth softly opened beneath his, welcoming his exploration.

Alexei lifted his head suddenly, as though startled by the impact of their contact. Without saying anything, he kissed her again, more deeply, pulling her body tightly against his until she could feel his desire pressing against her. Kendall trembled with her own. Her hands found their way inside his shirt so that she could trail her fingertips over his smoothly muscled chest and around to his back, reveling in the texture of his skin. She wanted to feel it bare against hers.

But then a little corner of Alexei's mind took control. He suddenly pulled away from her. "No, Kendall. We can't do this."

She gazed at him in the moonlight. "Why? We're both consenting adults."

Alexei's eyes took in the vision of her standing there, mussed and lovely, her cheeks faintly flushed. "We are. And I do want you." He shook his head and exhaled a long breath. "Oh, I do want you. But nothing is going to happen between the two of us. Not now. Not ever."

"I don't understand."

"This is where using my head over my heart comes in." He reached out and touched her warm cheek. "Kendall, you would be an easy woman for any man to fall in love with."

"Any man but you?"

"Including me. But I don't want to fall in love with you. Any kind of relationship between us could only end in tragedy and I'm not going to let that happen."

"It wouldn't have to."

"How could it be otherwise? Superficially we simply come from different countries, but the differences between us go much deeper. So deep that they're an intrinsic part of us. Historically, politically, socially—and personally. I have my life and you have yours, and those lives are destined to run along separate paths."

"But . . ."

Kendall started to say something, but Alexei lightly touched his fingers to her mouth. "Sshhh. Let's not talk any more tonight. Come on," he said as he took her hand in his. "It's time for me to take you home."

In silence they walked to their horses. Alexei gave her a boost onto Jasmine, then pulled himself onto Rocky's back. Again in silence, the two of them rode back and stabled the horses. He walked her to the front door and stood looking down at her lovely face. Leaning toward her, he gently pressed his mouth against her forehead. "Good night, Kendall Stuart."

He reached past her and picked up his briefcase, then walked to his car and drove away without looking back.

Kendall closed her front door and leaned her back against it. Hera walked over to her at that moment, as though realizing her mistress needed to be comforted, and rubbed against her. Kendall leaned over and wrapped her arms around the dog. "Oh, Hera," she said, her cheek against the animal's head, "what have I done?"

Alexei drove for a few miles, then suddenly pulled his car off the road and just sat there. "Damn," he finally said as he struck his fist against the steering wheel.

Chapter Four

Two weeks later—two weeks of not having heard from Alexei—Kendall was sitting in her office staring out the window when Ginny walked in. Shaking her head, Ginny sat down across from her and propped her feet up on the desk. "Hard at work again, I see."

Kendall turned in a daze, as though just realizing that someone was there. "What?"

"Nothing important." Ginny studied her friend with a worried frown. "What's wrong with you lately?"

"I guess I've been a little preoccupied."

"A little? Talk about understatement!"

"All right," Kendall admitted. "A lot."

"May I ask why?"

"You can ask, but I don't think I'm ready to talk about it yet."

"It has something to do with Alexei Demyenov, doesn't it?"

Kendall focused on her friend. "What makes you say that?"

"Because you've been like this since you met him."

"Have I?" she asked absently.

"Yes, dear, you have."

Kendall sighed.

"There it is again."

"There what is?"

"The incredible sigh. Sometimes I can hear it down in my office."

"Oh, you can't."

"Well, all right," Ginny conceded, "but I almost can." She'd never seen her friend like this and it disturbed her. "Is there a problem?"

"You might say that. In fact, you probably *would* say that. I think I've fallen in love with the man."

Ginny stared at her for a full thirty seconds with her mouth slightly open. "How could you do something so careless?"

"It just happened," Kendall said softly. "There was no warning."

"How does Alexei feel?"

"He's attracted to me, but I don't think it goes any deeper than that. As he told me the night we had dinner, I lead with my heart, he leads with his head."

"Have you talked to him since that night?"

Kendall shook her head.

"Well," Ginny said trying to sound efficient, "you'll just have to get over him."

Kendall looked her friend in the eye. "All right. Now, you tell me how."

Ginny lifted her shoulders. "I don't know. I just know that he's right to step back and now you have to do the same thing. Put your feelings behind you and move on."

Kendall swiveled her chair slightly and stared out the window again. "That sounds good, but I just don't know how to do that. What I feel for Alexei isn't something I have any control over."

Ginny, feeling helpless, walked behind Kendall's chair and lightly touched her friend's shoulder. "I know it's early but you're not doing yourself or the office any good today. Go home, ride your horses, commune with nature, do whatever you have to in order to feel better."

Kendall didn't say anything for a few moments, then she emitted a sigh that sounded as though it came from her toes and she patted Ginny's hand. "Thanks. I think I will."

Without saying anything else, she picked up her purse and left.

As Kendall pulled into her driveway, she stopped short. The gate was wide open. She knew she'd closed it that morning. Driving slowly through, her car crept the distance to the house. The dogs, who'd been let out that morning, were nowhere to be found. That frightened her more than anything because she knew that even with an open gate they'd never leave the property.

Kendall climbed out of her car and stood there. "Hera! Sniff! Jangles! Here, girls!"

There was nothing but silence.

She looked at her house. The front door gaped open like a surprised mouth. Walking around her car, Kendall went slowly up the steps and stood in the doorway. An involuntary gasp escaped her lips. It was a mess. As she walked farther in, she saw couch cushions scattered across the floors; books stripped from shelves; vases overturned and shattered; drawers pulled out and upended, the contents heaped ignominiously on the floor.

Police. She had to call the police. Even as she began searching for the phone, it rang. She followed the sound and found it buried under a cushion, the receiver still miraculously attached. Almost in a daze, she picked it up. "Hello."

"Kendall? This is Alexei. I tried to call you at the office, but your partner told me you'd be home. I just got word that the conference has been approved."

There was a long silence.

"Kendall?"

"Alexei . . ." Her hand clutched the phone.

"What's wrong?"

"Someone's been here." Her appalled eyes roamed over the destruction. "My home . . ."

"My God. And you're in it?"

"Yes. I just . . ."

"Get out. Get out right now. Get in your car and drive off the property."

"No one's here. There's no other car."

"That doesn't mean anything. I want you to promise me that you'll leave. I'm going to call the police."

"I have to find my dogs."

"You will. We will. But not until help arrives. Now hang up the phone and do what I told you."

His urgency finally penetrated. She quickly hung up, ran back out to her car, then drove to just outside the fence and sat there, her eyes searching in vain for some sign of the dogs.

It seemed like forever but was in fact only ten minutes before the police arrived. She started to follow them in but was waved back, and once again she had to sit still. When she was finally allowed back in, she entered with something akin to dread. Very slowly she went through the house room by room, calling her dogs, finally walking out through the back door.

Kendall nearly tripped over them. Three big, beautiful bundles of fur lying completely still. She dropped to her knees next to Hera. "Oh, no. Oh, no." She lifted Hera's head and set it gently in her lap, stroking it.

"Kendall!" Alexei's voice called to her from within the house.

"Out here," she finally managed to say after her second try.

Alexei stood in the doorway.

Kendall looked up at him with tears streaming down her cheeks. "Look at what they did. Look at what they did."

His heart was in his eyes as he joined her on the porch. He kneeled down and ran his hand over the fur of one of the puppies. Then curiously did it again.

There was movement. Sniff, at least, was breathing. It was shallow, but it was breath. He did the same thing to Jangles and then Hera, then looked at Kendall. "They aren't dead. Call their doctor."

Kendall dashed into the house and made the call, then ran back out again so she could check them herself. "Are you sure?"

He took her hand and placed it on Hera's chest. She felt the slight movement. "Oh, thank God."

"My guess is that they've been tranquilized."

Kendall's hand had been stroking Hera, but now it grew still. "Tranquilized? That doesn't sound like the work of some common burglar."

"They could have put something in some meat."

Kendall shook her head. "My dogs won't take food from strangers. Only my family, my neighbor and the people who work at the veterinary clinic."

"Maybe, just this once..."

"No. They wouldn't. And it can't have been injection because no one could have gotten close enough for that." Her eyes met his. "Do you suppose whoever it was could have used a tranquilizer gun?"

"Nothing else makes any sense."

"Miss Stuart?" a policeman said as he looked at her through the screen door. "I'd appreciate it if you'd come in. We need to ask you a few questions."

Kendall glanced worriedly at her dogs.

Alexei saw the look and reached out to touch her arm. "I'll look after them. You go ahead."

With a shaky smile that tugged at his heart, she went into the house.

Alexei felt like the worst kind of traitor. He had no proof, but he felt he knew who was behind this.

An hour later when she'd finished with the policemen, she walked onto the back porch. The vet was giving the dogs a very thorough once-over while Alexei did what he could to help. She kneeled next to them. "Are they going to be all right, Dr. Ferin?"

He shook his great white head in a way that reminded her of Hemingway. "I'll tell you, Kendall, it's the damnedest thing I've ever seen."

"But they're going to be all right?"

He patted her knee reassuringly. "Their vital signs are a little weak, but I don't think that's anything that won't be overcome when the tranquilizer wears off. I want to take them back to the clinic with me so we can keep an eye on them throughout the night."

Kendall nodded.

"I also want to take some blood samples to see if we can't isolate exactly what we're dealing with here." He got to his feet and looked at Alexei. "You look healthy. Help me get these girls to my van."

Alexei scooped Hera into his arms and lifted her as easily as a doll. Dr Ferin picked up Sniff and while the two men walked through the house to the van, Kendall stayed with Jangles. Alexei returned after only a few minutes and took Jangles. Kendall followed him to the van, taking a last look at her dogs to make sure they were comfortable.

"I'll call you first thing in the morning," the doctor told her as he climbed into the driver's seat. "And don't worry about them. They'll be fine."

As the doctor drove away with the dogs, Alexei suddenly turned Kendall into his arms and held her close. "The doctor said that they'll be fine."

She rested her cheek on his strong shoulder. "I know."

He stroked her silky hair. "Oh, Kendall," he said softly, "I'm so sorry."

"I hate to go back inside."

"Are you afraid?"

"Not right now, but I imagine that's going to change later, when I'm alone. For the moment I just don't think I can face the mess."

"I'll help you clean it up."

"You don't have to do that."

"I know I don't have to, but I want to."

The police came outside at that moment. The one who'd asked her to look around earlier approached. "Miss Stuart?"

She reluctantly left the sanctuary of Alexei's arms. "Yes?"

"We've done all we can on site. If and when we come up with anything conclusive, we'll let you know, but I have to tell you that I can't figure out why nothing was taken. It doesn't make sense for someone to go to all this trouble and walk away with nothing—unless whoever it was was looking for something very specific."

"I know." She extended her hand. "Thank you. I appreciate everything you've done."

"No problem. If you find during cleanup that we've overlooked something, let us know."

As the police cars drove off, Kendall turned to Alexei. "Well, we might as well get started."

They walked into the house together. Kendall sighed as she looked around the living room. "It's hard to know where to start."

"I think if we get the books back on the shelves first we'll at least be able to cross the room without too much trouble." He picked up an armful and headed for one of the bookcases. "Do you want them organized in any particular way?"

"No. I can take care of that another time. Just get them put away." She started on the furniture cushions, digging them out from under the rest of the mess and brushing them off before putting them in place.

They spent the rest of the evening working together, moving from room to room, saving the dining room for last, perhaps because it was the least damaged. Kendall didn't have expensive china or silver, so she assumed that nothing of any particular value was broken. The tablecloths and napkins had been taken from their drawers and scattered on the floor. She saw something shiny under a corner of one of the napkins. Leaning over, she moved the linen aside and saw a very lovely, very old and very shattered crystal sugar bowl. She sat on the carpeting next to it and tenderly picked up the sharp pieces.

Alexei, who had been watching her, walked over to where she sat and bent down beside her. "What is it?"

She held one of the pieces out to him. "Shattered crystal. It used to be my grandmother's sugar bowl." Kendall shook her head. "I don't understand why anyone would do something like this. What was the point of hurting my dogs and ransacking my home?''

Alexei took the pieces of broken bowl from her hands and set them on a chair, then pulled her into his arms and held her. "I think," he said softly, his mouth moving against her silky hair, "that this was directed at me, not you."

Kendall pulled slightly away from him but was still within the circle of his arms. Her eyes rested quizzically on his. "Do you know who did this, Alexei?"

"I think I do."

"Who?"

"I can't tell you that, but I promise you it'll never happen again."

"Does it have something to do with your seeing me?"

He kissed her forehead and pulled her back into his arms. Her cheek rested on his shoulder. "It has to do with the *reason* I'm supposed to be seeing you."

"Oh. You mean getting information from me about my father."

Alexei had been stroking her hair. His hand suddenly stopped in midair. "What do you know about that?"

She raised her head and smiled at him. "Surprised?"

"You could say that."

"I had some government visitors who warned me about you."

"And yet you continued seeing me." He gazed into her gray eyes. "Why?"

"Because I knew they were wrong."

"And how did you know?"

Kendall raised her hand to his face and traced the groove in his cheek with her fingertip. She knew without reservation that what she felt for this man, whether he ever returned her love or not, was something that would always be within her. "Because I love you," she said softly, "and I could never love a man who was less than honorable."

Alexei's heart sank at her words. He caught her hand in his. "Oh, Kendall Stuart, do you have any idea what you're saying?"

"I know," she said softly. "I'm telling you what I feel; what I've felt since I met you."

Alexei sighed as he rested his forehead against hers and looked into her eyes. "I knew you were going to be trouble the minute I saw you."

She didn't say anything.

"You know, don't you, that there can't be any kind of relationship between us?"

"I don't know that at all."

He moved away from her. "Kendall, look at me." She did, her heart in her eyes.

"What do you see?"

"A man."

"A Russian. And no matter how long I live in your country, I'll still be a Russian."

"But you *are* living here now."

"For how long? A few more months? Years? Then what?"

"You can ask to stay on. Or I could move to Russia to be with you."

"I would never be allowed to stay here. Certainly not because of a woman. And as for you moving to Russia," he shook his head, "you'd wither away there."

"Surely in this day and age..."

"Kendall, I know what I'm talking about. So we're back to the original question. What will we do when I leave?"

"We'll deal with that when the time comes."

Alexei shook his head. "No. We'll deal with that now." He took her chin between his thumb and forefinger and raised her eyes to his. "I don't want what you feel for me to turn into a tragedy in your life."

"That won't happen."

"It could if we let things between us go any further."

Kendall gazed at him in her quiet way. "Is this your polite way of saying that you don't feel anything where I'm concerned?"

His dark eyes softened. "I feel more than I want to. More than I expected to. Being with you has been like going on a voyage of discovery. I don't want it to stop, Kendall. But it has to. I don't want us to fall in love with each other only to have to part in the end."

"But at least when it ends we'll have had some time together. This way it stops before it begins."

"That's the way it has to be." He rose and looked down at her. "I wish there was some other way."

Kendall held out her hand and Alexei helped her to her feet. Without saying anything, she walked into his arms and sighed as his strength closed around her.

He inhaled the fragrant scent of her hair and closed his eyes as he rested his mouth against the silky strands. For a long moment, neither of them said anything. Then Alexei opened his eyes and with his hands on Kendall's shoulders held her away from him. "You've had a very long and traumatic day." His fingers gently traced a shadow beneath her eye. "Why don't you go on to bed? I'll finish up here."

Kendall looked around the dining room. "I can't leave you with this."

"There really isn't that much. It should only take another half an hour. And then I have some things that need to be taken care of at the embassy. I'll make sure someone is here to watch over you before I leave."

"That's not necessary."

"I don't want you here alone, Kendall. I'll have Sergei sit in his car outside your gate."

"I'm sure he'll love that," she said dryly.

"He's a good man. You can trust him. Now, my beautiful gray-eyed American, get yourself to bed. I'll talk to you tomorrow."

Kendall looked at him for a moment, then suddenly leaned forward and lightly brushed her mouth against his. "Good night, Alexei."

Alexei wanted nothing better than to pull her into his arms and hold her tightly, but he kept his hands at his sides. "Good night."

As soon as Kendall was up the steps, he called Sergei and told him what was going on, then he finished picking up the dining room. Turning out the downstairs lights, Alexei started to leave. He had his hand on the doorknob. But then he stopped. He couldn't leave without at least seeing her. Very quietly, he went upstairs. The hall light was on. Her bedroom was the first door he tried. He gazed around the room in the dim light. A smile touched his mouth. It was a wonderful room. Large, and yet enclosing. There was an air of silence about it. And it smelled wonderful—like Kendall. He walked to the bed and stood looking down at her in the dim light that shone from the hallway. Her head lay on a white pillow edged with lace. She hugged a matching pillow in her arms.

Alexei shook his head as he brushed her hair away from her cheek. What was it about this woman that drew him so?

Air-conditioning had made the room cool. He pulled the summer blanket up and tucked it around her, then leaned over Kendall and kissed her cheek.

"I wish things could be different between us," he said softly.

As Alexei left the room and closed the door after him, a hot tear escaped from the corner of Kendall's eye and dropped onto her pillow.

Alexei made sure the house was locked and climbed into his car. As he drove through the gate, he spotted Sergei, already there, his cigarette glowing in the darkness. Alexei flashed his headlights to acknowledge his presence and headed back to take care of some unfinished business at the embassy.

As soon as he arrived, he went straight to the KGB agent's quarters and knocked. Boris opened the door. Alexei could see some people in the room behind him. He stepped slightly past the agent. "Please excuse us for a moment," he said politely to the guests, then with his hand on Boris's arm, pulled him into the hallway and closed the door behind them. With a sudden force that the agent wasn't expecting, Alexei grabbed Boris's shirt at the throat and slammed him up against the wall. His eyes were black with anger. "I was just at Kendall Stuart's home," he said in Russian.

The agent started to say something, but Alexei cut him off.

"I'm going to tell you this and I'm only going to say it once. You stay away from her, Breskov. If I find out that you've been anywhere near her, her home or her family again, you'll answer to me. Believe it." With that, Alexei released his grip on the agent and smoothed the man's wrinkled shirt with a gesture that was menacing in its very solicitousness. "And now," he said, "you may return to your guests."

When Alexei got to his own quarters, he paced back and forth like a caged animal. "Come!" he barked out at a knock on his door.

Ambassador Brodsky opened the door and looked in. "Alexei. I thought I heard you return but apparently my interruption is an untimely one."

"I'm sorry. Please, come in."

"Are you sure?"

"I'm sure. But I should warn you that I'm not very good company tonight, Fyodor."

"I'm not looking for good company," the ambassador said as he walked further into the room and closed the door behind him. "I thought you might need someone to talk to."

Alexei stopped pacing and looked at him curiously. "Why would you think that?"

"You haven't been yourself for the past few weeks," the ambassador explained as he sank into a chair. "Talk to me about it, Alexei."

"There's nothing to say."

The ambassador picked up a book from the end table. "Yevtuschenko," he said. "You should be more careful of the books you leave lying around." As he went to put it back on the table, it fell off and landed on the floor. When the ambassador leaned over to pick it up, a white rose fell from between the pages. He looked at it for a long moment before picking it up and sliding it carefully back into the book. "My friend," he said, "something—or someone—has been on your mind. I know it and you know it. Talk to me. Maybe I can help."

Alexei paced back and forth a few more times, then sat on the edge of a chair across from the ambassador. "My problem—if a problem is what I have—is a woman."

The older man glanced out of the corner of his eye at the book with the rose in it. "I see."

"I've fallen in love."

"With an American?"

"Yes," he said quietly.

"Then a problem is definitely what you have, Alexei. How does the young woman in question feel?"

"The same."

"What are you going to do about it?"

"I don't know. I honestly don't know." Alexei sighed tiredly and leaned back in his chair.

"You could have an affair with her and try to get her out of your system."

Alexei shook his head. "She's not the kind of woman a man could get out of his system. She's in mine and she's there for life."

"So what are you saying? That you want to marry this American?"

Alexei was silent for a moment. "I guess I am."

"Is she aware of your feelings?"

"Not the depth of them, no."

"That's good. If she doesn't know, she won't be encouraged. There are too many problems involved in this kind of relationship."

"Do you think I haven't thought of that, Fyodor? I know about all of the pitfalls. I've gone over them in my mind again and again, and God help me, it changes nothing. I love her."

The ambassador sighed.

"I've been thinking about this for weeks now, almost since the day I met her, and I think the answer is to go directly to the government and ask their permission for our marriage."

"They won't give it and you'll ruin your career in the process."

"I have to try something, Fyodor."

The ambassador shook his head. "No. This is no solution. I suggest you give yourself time away from the rose. You'll get over her."

"How do you get over someone who makes you feel whole when you're with her?"

"You'll get over her because you have no choice, Alexei." The ambassador studied Alexei in sympathetic silence. "I almost envy you," he finally said. "I've never in my life felt that way about another human being."

Alexei was silent.

"If you try to make some kind of arrangement so that you can be with this woman you claim to love, you will turn her life into a nightmare."

"I know that," he said quietly.

"Then please, Alexei, reconsider. For her sake as much as your own."

"I don't want to spend my life without her."

"You have no choice. And I'll tell you something else. You've accomplished a lot during your time here. You're helping to bring about change for the better. You have considerations here other than what you want. You must think about your country, your people. You're needed."

"I know."

"For you to throw it all away would be nothing short of a criminal act. I suggest that you consider a temporary transfer back to Moscow to get your bearings," the ambassador said as he got to his feet. "If I can be of any help, you know all you have to do is ask."

Alexei rose as well. "I know, Fyodor. And I thank you."

When the older man had gone, Alexei walked to his window and stared outside. There was a certain irony to this situation. Fate had brought him together with the woman he knew in his heart was meant for him, yet it was the fate of their births that was going to keep them apart.

Chapter Five

Alexei drove to Kendall's house early the next afternoon. It was very quiet this time with no dogs to greet him. Walking up the steps to the porch, he rang the bell and waited. There was no answer. Then he knocked and waited again. Still there was no answer.

"Can I help you?"

Alexei turned to find an old man standing about ten feet away from the porch, wiping his hands on a cloth and looking at him. "Who are you?"

"Name's Buddy Simpson. I'm a neighbor of Miss Stuart's. She isn't home right now."

"Do you know where she is?"

The man studied him hard from under bushy white eyebrows. "Sure do."

Alexei waited, but the man said nothing else. "Would you mind telling me where she is?" he finally asked.

"That all depends. Who are you?"

"My name is Alexei Demyenov. I'm a—friend—of Kendall's."

"You the fellow who put that guard on her last night?" He pointed to where Sergei was still sitting in his car.

"That's right."

The man watched him a little longer. "All right. She took one of the horses and rode out to the stream early this morning."

"You mean she hasn't come back yet?"

"That's right, but there's nothing to worry about. She does this all of the time."

"I'd like to go out and talk to her. Where's the other horse?"

"Rocky's in the stables. I don't suppose she'd mind if you took him."

Alexei, dressed in a rough-textured summer suit the color of oatmeal, took off his jacket as he walked toward the stables and rolled up the sleeves of his shirt. He found Rocky in one of the stalls and led him out. Tossing his jacket onto a wooden peg, he pulled himself onto the unsaddled horse, headed out of the stables and into the pasture. Rocky, full of energy, galloped for the first few minutes, then slowed down to a comfortable gait.

As soon as they got to the stream, Alexei spotted Kendall. She'd spread a blanket out under a tree and was lying on it. He rode the horse quietly through the stream and dismounted about twenty feet away from her. Alexei patted Rocky on the rump and the horse trotted over to where Jasmine was grazing while Alexei walked toward Kendall. She lay on her back with her head slightly propped up, a book open next to her, her eyes closed. He lowered himself onto the blanket beside her and just let his eyes drink in everything about her. She was wearing a short white culotte-like skirt that came only halfway down her long, tanned thighs and a cool white knit shirt tucked in at the waist with a wide pink belt in the middle.

For the next hour, very quietly, he just watched her.

She moved a little, sighed and stretched her arms high over her head. After a moment, Kendall opened her eyes and found herself looking at Alexei. A soft smile curved her mouth. "Good morning."

He reached out a gentle hand and pushed her hair away from her face. "Good afternoon."

"Afternoon?" She sat up and looked at her watch. "I had no idea I'd been here that long." Her eyes moved to his. "What are you doing here?"

"Watching you. How are your dogs?"

"I called the doctor this morning and he said they're still groggy, but otherwise just fine. He's going to keep them until tomorrow."

"Good."

Kendall, fully awake now, looked at Alexei closely. "Did you get any sleep last night?"

"Not much."

"What's wrong?"

"I'm going back to the Soviet Union."

Kendall blinked at the unexpectedness of his words. "Why?"

"A lot of reasons, the main one being that I have things to do there."

Kendall didn't believe him. "No," she said, shaking her head. "You're leaving because of me."

"Partly," Alexei agreed quietly, "and partly because of me."

"Are you coming back to Washington?"

"Yes. Whenever I'm needed."

"What about your job here?"

"I still have it. I just won't be living here."

"When did you decide that?"

"First thing this morning." Alexei trailed the back of his fingers down her cheek. "Don't look at me like that, Kendall." His hand moved around to stroke the back of her neck.

"I don't know how else to look."

"It's for the best."

Her eyes met his. "If you think that vanishing from my life is going to make me love you less, you're very, very wrong, Alexei."

"Give yourself time."

"Time to do what?" she asked softly. "Stop loving you? Time has nothing to do with this. Neither does distance." She lightly touched his arm. "Alexei, if you're leaving Washington because of me, please don't. I probably shouldn't have said anything to you about what I was feeling, but now that I have, you should also know that I can handle rejection. It hurts like hell, and it doesn't change how I feel about you, but I can handle it."

A corner of his mouth lifted. "Rejection? The last thing in the world I want to do is reject you."

A small frown creased her forehead. "I don't understand."

"The only way I'm going to be able to stay away from you is to leave here and put myself in a place where I have no choice."

"But..."

He touched his fingers to her mouth. "I've thought about all of the options. This is the best thing for both of us. There can never be any kind of relationship between the two of us. Not ever."

Kendall's eyes burned with the tears she was holding back. "I'm not going to see you again, am I?" Kendall asked quietly.

"No."

Six weeks later, Kendall walked into a restaurant and looked around. Ginny stood up and waved as Kendall made her way through the crowded room to her table. "Hi," she said breathlessly as she sat down. "Have you been waiting long?"

"Just got here. I ordered us both iced tea."

"Perfect."

"How'd it go with the Russians?"

"Fine. They're doing what we expected with their conference participants, though."

"Hard-liners?"

"Very."

"Is that going to be a problem?"

"I hope not, but we won't know for sure until December."

"I suppose." Ginny looked closely at her friend. "Did you run into anyone in particular while you were at the embassy?"

"By anyone in particular I assume you mean Alexei."

"I might."

"No. But I heard he was back for the television debate tonight."

"Are you going to see him?"

"No."

"Are you all right, Kendall?"

"I'm just fine. Can we talk about something else?"

Ginny knew her friend wasn't fine. She hadn't been for a long time.

Alexei had looked up from his menu to see Kendall walking across the room. He was about fifteen feet away, but he had a perfect view of her as she sat across the table from her partner.

Ambassador Brodsky watched the expression on Alexei's face and then turned in his chair to see what had caused it. "So," he said after a moment, "that's your rose."

Alexei tore his eyes away from Kendall and looked back at his menu. "Yes."

"She's lovely."

"What do you feel like eating today, Fyodor?"

"Nothing at the moment. I'd prefer talking to you about your lady."

"She's not my lady."

"Not in fact but in your heart. I take it from the way you looked at her that going back to the Soviet Union hasn't helped."

Alexei put down his menu. With a will of their own, his eyes went back to Kendall just as she smiled at something Ginny said. His heart skipped a beat. "That's right."

"Coming back here was a mistake."

"I had no choice."

"Does anyone besides me know about her?"

"No."

"Good. It's best if it stays that way. Your movements could become severely restricted."

"I understand that."

The ambassador studied the younger man in silence. "She has quite a hold over you."

Alexei said nothing.

Kendall suddenly sensed that she was being watched. She hesitated for just a moment, then raised her gaze until she found herself looking directly into a pair of familiar dark brown eyes. Pain flashed in her expression. It was brief, but undeniably there.

Alexei felt the contact of that look. He wanted to go to her, but he remained seated.

Kendall shouldered her purse and turned to Ginny. "I'm sorry, but I can't stay for lunch."

Ginny looked at her in surprise. "What?"

"I have to go."

"But you just got here," she said in exasperation.

"I know, but I have some things to do. I just remembered."

"All right. Do you want me to bring something back to the office for you?"

"No, thanks. I don't have much of an appetite."

"Kendall..."

But the name was uttered too late. Kendall was already out of her chair and halfway across the room.

Alexei started to rise, but the ambassador put his hand on Alexei's shoulder to hold him in his seat. "Let her go," he said firmly.

Alexei's whole body had tensed, but he slowly released it.

"That's better. Now let's have some lunch."

Kendall worked until well into the evening. It was dark outside when she finally got home. The three dogs greeted her with barks and wagging tails and followed her into the house. She went straight through to the kitchen and poured herself a white wine, then carried it into the living room and kicked off her high heels before sinking into her favorite chair.

She looked at her watch and then at the empty television screen. Almost defiantly, she picked up a book she'd started a few days before and opened it. But opening it and reading it were two different things. Her eyes took in the words but her mind couldn't comprehend their meaning.

After fifteen minutes, she closed the book and sat there tapping her fingers on its hard cover. Should she or shouldn't she?

Kendall picked up the remote control and pressed the on button. The television flashed to life and there, before her eyes, was Alexei. Hera, as though recognizing her friend's voice, barked. Kendall moved closer to the screen and sat cross-legged on the floor.

The camera moved away from him and panned over the journalists seated at a semicircular table. This was precisely the setup Kendall and Ginny had been using with their conferences, taping them over a period of ten days and then releasing them as documentaries. The moderator, a Harvard law professor, moved within that semicircle, asking first one panelist a question and then another, always coming back to Alexei to rebut. It was an informal and yet remarkably informative type of debate. Alexei articulated his points beautifully. His arguments were well-reasoned and thoughtful. He never took the hard line that many Americans had come to expect of Soviets, but trod a path somewhere in the middle, able to see both sides of an issue without being blinded by any kind of anti-American sentiment.

The Soviets couldn't have picked a better spokesman.

Kendall watched until it was over, then reached for her remote control and clicked the television off. Lying back on the floor with a sigh, she automatically wrapped her arm around Hera when the dog came to lie beside her. "Why does everything have to be so complicated?" she asked.

Hera licked her hand and Kendall smiled softly. "Except you."

She turned her head and stared at the ceiling. There had been an ache deep within her for a long time and she didn't see an end to it any time soon.

"Tell me, Hera, how long does it take to stop loving someone?"

The dog didn't answer.

There was no answer.

Kendall lay in bed, not sleeping but tossing from side to side. She kept thinking of how close Alexei was. So close, and yet he might as well have been in Moscow.

The phone rang. Kendall looked at the illuminated face of her bedside clock. It was after two in the morning. Reaching across her pillow, she picked up the receiver. "Hello."

"Hello, Kendall."

She clutched the receiver in both hands and sank back onto the pillow. "Alexei."

"I know it's late. I'm sorry."

"No. It's all right."

"I'm going back to Moscow tomorrow."

"I know. I heard some people talking while I was in your embassy this morning. How are things there?"

"Fine. I'm teaching some courses at Moscow University and giving lectures on American culture, of all things. How have you been?"

"All right. I—watched you on television tonight. You held your own nicely, as usual."

"Thank you." He paused. "Kendall, when I saw you at the restaurant today, you seemed to have lost weight."

"Just a little. I always do in the summer."

"Are you taking care of yourself?"

She nodded, then realized he couldn't see her. "Yes. Whenever I forget to eat, Ginny reminds me."

"Tell her to keep up the good work."

"I wouldn't dream of it. She'll only be encouraged." Kendall paused. "Will I be seeing you before you go back?"

"No. I probably shouldn't even have called, but I wanted to hear your voice."

"I'm glad you did." Kendall swallowed hard. "I wanted to hear yours, too."

"Good night, Kendall," he said softly. "Have sweet dreams."

"Good night, Alexei."

Both of them sat there for a moment, neither willing to be the one to break the connection. Finally, Kendall put the receiver in its cradle. She lay back against her pillow once more and exhaled a shaky breath.

Alexei, still in the dark suit he'd worn to a dinner that evening, listened for a moment as the line went dead then replaced his own receiver. "Oh, Kendall," he said quietly. "Why can't I get you out of my heart?"

Chapter Six

It was ten o'clock at night when the plane finally circled once over the lighted Moscow airport and landed. There was no exit ramp that snaked out from the terminal to the plane, so everyone bundled up in his coat to prepare for the walk across the tarmac. The icy wind hit Kendall full-face and made her gasp as she lowered her head and forged on. Ginny was right behind her.

A woman opened the door for the two of them and their group of ten and ushered them into a waiting room. In her thickly accented English, she asked them to wait, and then she left. Kendall and Ginny looked at each other and shrugged. There were no chairs or windows in the room so everyone stood around chatting quietly among themselves. After a while the group of dignified men and women Kendall had gathered together for this conference began sitting on the floor, their backs against the wall.

Kendall looked at Ginny. "This is ridiculous."

"I wonder what the delay is."

"I don't know, but I'm going to find out." Kendall opened the door and went into the hall. She was stopped not ten feet from the door by a uniformed man who pointed his finger and ordered her back in no uncertain terms. When Kendall tried to explain to him that they were all tired and wanted to go to their hotel, he lowered his brows at her and jabbed his finger toward the room she'd just left.

Still feeling a need to cooperate, Kendall did as she was told, but when another hour had passed, she went back out. The same guard made the same gesture. This time Kendall stood her ground. "I want to see whoever is in charge."

He surprised her by speaking in English. "Go back where you were. Someone will be with you in time."

"We've been waiting for nearly two hours."

"We're aware of how long you've been waiting."

"Then I'd like something to be done about it now."

He looked her up and down. "Go back."

"No. Not until I've spoken with someone in authority."

"I am in authority."

Kendall sighed in frustration. She was exhausted. "Look," she explained patiently, "we've been traveling for a long time. All we want is the courtesy of an explanation as to why we're being delayed like this."

"You will receive one in time. Now, go back."

His refusal to cooperate only served to make her more determined. "I'll go back after I've spoken with someone who has a reasonable explanation for the delay."

The officer signaled to another officer. The other one approached and the two men conversed in Russian for a moment. "You will go with him," the one who spoke English told her. "You will go with him now."

"At last," Kendall said gratefully. "Thank you."

Ginny watched nervously from the doorway as Kendall was led away until the guard who remained behind shooed her back into the room and closed the door.

Kendall was taken to another small, windowless room, this one also without furniture. She paced back and forth for awhile, glancing at her watch every few minutes. When half an hour had gone by, she tried to open the door to find out what was going on, but it was locked. She pulled and pulled, but nothing happened. She even tried knocking on it with her fist. "Hello? Is anyone there?"

There was no answer.

She tried jiggling the knob again but the door wouldn't budge. Nothing helped.

"Hello?" she called, pounding harder.

Still there was no answer.

Stepping back, her heart racing, Kendall looked around. She'd always had this fear of small, enclosed places. She'd overcome it to a great extent as she'd gotten older, but sometimes, like now, when there were no windows and no way out, she could feel that horrible panic welling up inside her.

She shivered and rubbed her hands up and down her arms. They wouldn't just leave her in here, would they?

Taking a deep breath, she forced herself to exhale slowly and calmly. Pacing wasn't helping.

Kendall refused to let the panic overwhelm her. Leaning against the wall, she slid to the floor and hugged her knees to her breast. Closing her eyes tightly, she used a little trick her father had taught her when she was a child and imagined herself outside at her home, gazing around at the wide, open spaces. After a few minutes it got easier and the panic subsided.

How long she sat like that, Kendall didn't know, but it had to have been hours. She was so far off in her imagination that when the door finally opened she wasn't even aware of it.

When Alexei walked in, his eyes softened at the sight of her huddled in the corner. "Kendall?" he said softly.

She opened her eyes and blinked, sure she'd dreamed that wonderful voice. "Alexei?"

Crossing the small cubicle, he held out his hand and helped her to her feet. Kendall walked straight into his arms and buried her face in his shoulder. He held her trembling body tightly to his for a moment.

"Get me out of here," she whispered against the cloth of his coat. "Please."

Alexei's response was to put his arm around her and walk her out the door past the soldier who was standing there. He said something in Russian and kept walking. As they were about to leave, Alexei removed his heavy coat and draped it around Kendall's shoulders. "All of your things are at the hotel," he explained.

"What about you?" Kendall asked as she looked at the pale yellow cable-knit sweater he had on.

"I'm fine."

They started through the door, but Kendall stopped suddenly. "My group. I was so happy to be out of there myself that I almost forgot them."

"Ginny and the rest of them are safely in their rooms at the hotel."

"When did that happen?"

"A few hours ago. They were held here at the airport for a while after you left with the soldier, but as soon as they cleared customs they were taken to the hotel."

Alexei, his arm around Kendall, walked her from the warmth of the airport into the icy night air and tucked her into his nearby car. He climbed in the driver's side and started the engine to give them some heat. "Are you hungry?"

Kendall had to think for a moment. "Yes, I am."

"I know a little café that stays open all night. We'll go there and have a sandwich."

Kendall turned in her seat and studied Alexei's profile as the car began moving forward. "Not that I'm complaining, mind you, but how did you find out I was still at the airport?"

"As soon as Ginny got back to the hotel, she paid one of the employees there to find me and tell me what had happened." He reached across the seat and took her cold hand in his. "I'm sorry I didn't get there sooner."

"I'm just glad you got there at all. Why did they do that to me?"

A corner of his mouth lifted. "Believe me, there was no sinister plot involved. The soldier you first spoke with didn't know what else to do with you. He's not used to people disobeying him. So he had you put in that room and then when he went off-duty you were forgotten."

Kendall shook her head and pulled the coat more tightly around her. "And there I was waiting to be grilled about heaven knows what. I hope they don't make a habit of that."

"We're not as bad as you think, Kendall. A little disorganized, perhaps."

"Is that what was taking so long at the airport?"

"That's one of the reasons. The other one is that every piece of luggage coming off the plane gets hand-searched item by item. Mechanical things are sometimes even taken apart and put back together."

"They did that without the owners being present?"

"That's the way it's done here sometimes. Especially with large groups such as yours."

Kendall studied his profile and didn't say anything for a long time.

Alexei turned his head and glanced at her. "What's wrong?"

"Nothing's wrong. I was just thinking how nice it is to see you again."

His eyes locked with hers for just a moment and then he turned his gaze back to the road. "It's good to see you, too, Kendall."

The two were silent for the rest of the drive. Kendall looked out the window, fascinated by their surroundings—or at least by what she could see of them. There was a building with a glass front that looked as though it housed offices. Windows had been strategically lit in such a way that they spelled out CCCP.

Alexei parked the car and walked around to help Kendall out. The wind had picked up considerably and both of them lowered their heads to battle against it as they ran into the small dark café. There were only eight tables. Alexei led her across the wood floor to the rear of the room and pulled out a chair for her. "What would you like?" he asked as he sat across from her.

"Hot chocolate."

"And to eat?"

"Just a sandwich. Any kind."

A large man in a clean white shirt walked over to the table and greeted Alexei by his first name.

"Kendall," Alexei said in English, "I'd like you to meet Yuri. He runs this place."

Kendall shook the man's hand and smiled an acknowledgment. Then Alexei placed their order. As soon as the man had left, he turned his attention back to Kendall. "Are you sure you're all right?"

"I'm fine. Just a little shaken. Nothing like that has ever happened to me before." Her eyes drank in the sight of him. "I wasn't expecting to see you on this trip."

"If Ginny hadn't contacted me, you wouldn't have."

"Oh."

"And once I get you back to the hotel, if I have my way, we won't see each other again."

Kendall lowered her eyes.

Alexei reached out with a gentle hand, taking her chin between his thumb and forefinger. "It's for the best."

"I know. But I should tell you that being away from you hasn't changed my feelings."

His eyes met hers and held as his hand fell away. "Nor has it mine."

Kendall caught her lower lip between her teeth and tried to look anywhere but at Alexei.

He reached across the table, covered her cold hand with his warm, strong one and squeezed reassuringly. "We'll get through this, and go on from here. So," he said, changing the subject, "how are your animals?"

She saw what he was doing and did her best to cooperate. "The horses are fine and the dogs haven't had any residual effects from the tranquilizers, except that they're a little more leery of strangers now."

"More leery? That must make a fun evening for your guests."

"Well," she said with a soft smile, "it's interesting. At least for the first fifteen minutes or so."

His eyes roamed over her lovely face, gathering memories for future reference. Her skin, even in winter, managed to have a healthy glow. Her gray eyes still sparkled. And the dimple he'd noticed at the corner of her mouth still flashed charmingly. Alexei had spent the past few months doing whatever he could to get Kendall out of his heart, but nothing had worked.

A smiling Yuri brought her a big mug of hot chocolate and set another of very black coffee in front of Alexei. Kendall, her eyes on Alexei, cupped the mug in both hands and raised it to her mouth. "Have you been seeing the woman you told me about?"

"Yes."

Kendall hesitated over the next question, but then decided to forge ahead. "Did you ever decide whether or not you were going to marry her?"

"I'm not."

Relief flooded through her. "Why?"

"Because I don't love her."

Kendall looked at him in surprise. "I was under the impression that love wasn't a requirement you had for a wife."

"It wasn't—in the past."

Yuri returned at that moment with a sandwich for Kendall. It looked like your basic American grilled cheese, which was just fine with her.

"What have you been doing with yourself since you left America?" she asked as she popped a finger-sized bite into her mouth.

"I've spent a lot of time in France and England doing basically the same work I did in America. Right now I'm teaching a course in law at Moscow University."

"It sounds like you have a full life."

"As full as it can be under the circumstances."

Suddenly Kendall lost her appetite and moved her plate away.

"What's wrong?"

She shook her head. "I want to spend the rest of the night sitting here with you, talking, looking at you, listening to the sound of your voice. But I know it has to end sometime."

"Would you like me to take you to your hotel now?"

"Yes, thank you."

He put some money on the table, then walked over to her as they rose and pulled his coat snugly around her. "Come on."

After he tucked her into his car, he walked around to the driver's side, but hesitated before opening the door.

"What is it?" Kendall asked when he finally got in next to her.

"Nothing."

But there was something. He looked into the rearview mirror as he started the engine and glanced into it periodically as he drove.

Kendall finally turned in her seat and looked behind them. There were only a couple of cars there, their headlights bright on the frigid night. Nothing out of the ordinary.

It only took them fifteen minutes to drive to the hotel, but it was a strangely tense time. When Alexei stopped his car in front of the pre-revolutionary building there was no one behind them, but he didn't seem to trust that.

He helped Kendall out of the car and into the hotel, then walked her up to the desk where a clerk was working. He smiled politely at Kendall and turned his attention to Alexei, who spoke to him in Russian. The clerk inclined his head and left, returning moments later with Kendall's passport in his hand.

"How did he get that?" she asked.

"Ginny."

She reached out her hand for it, but the clerk ignored her silent request, handing her instead an identification card and a key. "What's this?"

"Your passport will remain at the front desk during your stay here. For identification purposes in this hotel and around the city you'll need this card."

"I don't like the idea of turning over my passport."

"No one does, but it's a necessary evil. You'll find a concierge on your floor. If you need anything, ask him. And always, before you leave the hotel, turn your key over to him. And in case you're wondering, Ginny's in the room next to yours. Now you have everything you need."

Her eyes met his. "For the conference," she corrected.

"For the conference," he agreed. "I hope it's a good one for you."

"Thank you. And thank you for all your help tonight."

He looked as though he wanted to kiss her. Kendall knew she wanted him to. Instead she took his coat from around her shoulders and handed it back to him.

Without saying anything else, Alexei turned and walked away, slipping his arms into his coat as he moved.

She stood in the lobby watching him until he disappeared into the icy world beyond the doors.

No sooner had Alexei climbed into his car than the passenger door opened and another man slid in. Boris Breskov looked at Alexei with a smirk. "You can't stay away from her, can you?"

"What do you want?"

"I just thought I'd let you know that I'm watching you. That I'm always watching you."

"And exactly what is it you're hoping to see?"

"Oh, I'm not sure. Some little indiscretion. I'll know it when I see it. But more importantly, Demyenov, you'll know it when I see it."

Alexei said nothing.

"There I was in the United States trying to make you get information from her when what I should have been doing was watching to make sure that you weren't passing anything along to her."

"You know me better than that."

"I know you, and I've never liked or trusted you. You're up to something."

"The only thing I'm up to at the moment is trying to get home—which I could do if you'd get out of my car. You're wasting my time, Breskov."

"It's my time to waste." He lit a cigarette and smiled again at Alexei. "As I said, you're going to slip. I can smell it." He tapped his nose. "And when you do, I'm going to be there to catch you."

"It's generous of you to give me a warning."

"Not so generous. I know that even with a warning you're not going to be able to stay away from her. Kendall Stuart is your Achilles' heel, my friend. And

I'm aiming my arrow straight at it. Night after night you'll be going to bed alone, knowing that she's near. It was one thing when she was in America, but now she's so close you can smell her perfume."

The muscle in Alexei's jaw moved, but he remained silent.

Breskov laughed but there was no amusement in it. "Sweet dreams, Alexei." Without saying anything else, he got out of the car and climbed into his own immediately behind Alexei's.

Alexei sat still for a moment. Breskov was confident. Too confident. He was up to something. Slamming his car into gear, Alexei headed into the country, toward his new home on the Moscow River. A short time later, Breskov's car followed.

Kendall took the elevator to the fifth floor. As Alexei had told her to expect, there was indeed a concierge sitting behind a desk. In English, he requested her identification. She handed him the card she'd been given downstairs along with her room key. He studied the card closely, then returned it to her and waved her on.

Her room was at the very end of the long hall. The inside, in accordance with its pre-revolutionary standards, was large. The carpeting was so faded it was difficult to tell what the colors had been originally, and in spots it was worn threadbare, but the flowered pattern was still distinct. This had to be the original carpeting from the early 1900s. The bedspread matched the carpeting. It, too, was faded, and much-darned.

Still, there was a certain elegant aura of years gone by to the room that lent it a kind of sad charm.

Her two suitcases, purse and coat were set neatly in a corner. She hung up her coat and then mechanically began unpacking. She finished one suitcase and stopped. This was the last thing she wanted to do. Instead she went to her window and looked outside to see what kind of view she had.

Not a very good one, as it turned out. The street was full of buildings, some old, some new and grotesque-looking. She looked down at the street and was surprised to see that Alexei's car was still there. Another car had pulled in behind it. As she looked, a man got out of the passenger side of Alexei's car, pulled his collar up around his face to shield himself from the wind and stepped briskly off the curb and into his own car.

Kendall watched curiously. Had they been followed? Was that why Alexei had been looking into the rearview mirror? As she watched, Alexei's car pulled out. The car behind him waited a few moments and then also headed in the same direction.

She stayed at the window a little longer, but when nothing else happened she put her second suitcase on the bed and started unpacking it. As she lifted a sweater out, she paused at a sound she couldn't identify. "Kendall?" came a whispered voice through the door.

Kendall crossed the room and opened the door to find Ginny standing there in her nightgown. She quickly came in and closed the door behind her, then turned to Kendall and hugged her. "I'm so glad you're all right. I didn't know what was going on," she whispered.

"Why are you being so quiet?"

"That old fellow in the hall is sleeping." She shivered. "It's creepy having someone watch everything you do."

"In other words, you'd like him to stay asleep."

"Exactly." She walked over to Kendall's bed and sat cross-legged next to the suitcase. "So tell me what happened. What was going on? Where did they take you?"

"Just off to another room and then," she said dryly, "to show you how important I am, they apparently forgot I was there."

Ginny looked at her in disbelief. "You're kidding."

"No. I heard it straight from Alexei. And by the way, thanks for getting in touch with him. If you hadn't, I'd still be sitting there."

"I didn't know what else to do. It was either Alexei or the American embassy, and I figured we should keep things as low-key as possible."

"You did the right thing." Kendall continued taking things out of her suitcase and arranging them neatly in the dresser drawers.

"Oh, by the way, you had a note in your mailbox when we checked in telling us that we've been invited to a special cocktail party tomorrow night to meet our hosts and have our people introduced to their Soviet counterparts."

"What time?"

"Eight o'clock."

"Did you get a chance to look at the conference facilities in the hotel?"

"No. It was so late by the time we checked in that I just came up to my room."

"That's all right. We can do that tomorrow."

Ginny looked at her curiously. "Are you all right?"

Kendall looked up from what she was doing. "I'm fine. Why do you ask?"

"Well, I know it couldn't have been easy for you seeing Alexei tonight."

"Are you kidding? Seeing him was the easiest thing in the world. Letting him leave again was the hard part."

"Are you sure you're all right?"

This time Kendall smiled. "I'm sure. Stop worrying about me so much." She snapped her suitcase closed and set it inside the closet, then picked up her nightgown from the pillow where she'd placed it and carried it into the bathroom. "We should get an early start tomorrow morning and set things up since we won't be able to work very far into the evening. Was all of our video and sound equipment allowed through customs?"

"Yes, but heaven only knows what kind of shape it's in."

"What do you mean?"

"Well, if they took that stuff apart the way they did my hair dryer, we're in trouble."

Kendall looked around the corner as she slipped the nightgown over her head. "I hate to sound redundant, but what do you mean?"

"Let me put it this way—I went to dry my hair after I showered tonight and instead of blowing hot air out, it sucked my hair in."

Kendall laughed as she came out of the bathroom with a brush in her hand. "Well, if nothing else, this is going to be an interesting experience."

"And then some." Ginny unfolded her legs and got off the bed. "I'd love to talk longer, but I can't remember the last time I was so tired. I would have been asleep a long time ago, but I was worried about you."

Kendall gave her friend a hug. "I'm glad you came with me on this one."

"Just remember, you owe me. A big one." She went to the door and opened it wide enough to peer down the hall. "He's still asleep," she whispered. "Don't close your door all the way until I'm in my room."

Kendall went to the door and stood with her hand on the knob while she looked into the hall. The old concierge was tilted way back in his chair, his mouth drooping slightly open. Ginny tiptoed the short distance to her room, looked back at Kendall and grinned, then went into her room and closed her door with a soft click while Kendall did the same.

Flipping the wall switch, she plunged the room into darkness and climbed between the cold, clean sheets. It felt unbelievably good.

As she settled back against the pillows and grew still, the only sound she could hear was the wind howling past the windows. Every once in a while the glass actually rattled. Pulling the sheets up to her cold nose, Kendall slowly closed her eyes. Her last thought was of Alexei.

Chapter Seven

The air in the hotel was chilly, to say the least. The next morning, as Kendall wandered around the first-floor conference rooms making sure the video equipment was set up properly, she had on a pair of jeans and two sweaters but was still cold.

The Soviets, for their part, were setting up television equipment so that they could have live broadcasts of the conference. Tomorrow was the big day, and Kendall's nerves were telling on her. She was finding it difficult to get things done. This was either going to turn out to be a wonderful experience or one of the biggest bombs in her life.

A woman named Irina who'd been helping to set things up for the Soviets walked over to Kendall, a clipboard in her hands. "We will moderate tomorrow." There was no room for discussion in her tone of voice.

Kendall, her hands jammed into the pockets of her jeans to keep her fingers warm, looked at her in surprise. "No, that wasn't the agreement. I brought a moderator with me."

"I know what we agreed on previously, but we've changed our minds."

Kendall didn't want to be difficult. She really didn't. But she wasn't going to be walked over either. "You have to understand," Kendall explained patiently, "that the moderator sets the tone for the entire panel."

"We are aware of this fact."

"What we're looking for here is an equitable balance between East and West."

"We understand that also."

"At this point," Kendall said honestly, "I don't have very much faith in your side being able to do that. Your interests throughout these talks have been very self-serving."

"And yours have not?"

"That's right. I've worked hard at maintaining a balance of opinion among the people I selected to participate. The whole point of this is to share ideas, not propagandize."

"Then we must compromise."

Kendall had a sinking feeling that to this woman, compromise meant doing it her way. "Do you have something in mind?"

"Someone. We don't trust the man you've chosen to moderate, but we're willing to put up someone from our side for your approval."

"Who?"

"Alexei Demyenov."

Kendall's mouth opened softly. "Alexei?"

"Yes. You worked with him on this. You know that he is open-minded."

"Well, yes, I'm aware of that, but I don't think he'd agree to something like this."

"He already has." Irina held the clipboard to her chest and wrapped her large arms around it. "So what do you say?"

"Would it be possible for me to speak with him first?"

"Possible but unnecessary. You decide within the next hour and let me know." And with that she walked away, leaving a bemused Kendall staring after her.

Ginny walked over and looped her arm through Kendall's. "What was that all about?"

"They're already trying to change the rules."

"You knew to expect that."

"She wants Alexei to be the moderator."

"What?" Ginny squealed the word, and heads all over the room turned toward them. "We brought a man all the way here just for that purpose."

"Tell comrade Irina that."

"What does Alexei say?"

"According to her, he's agreed to do it."

"So where do we go from here?"

"I guess we let him do it. He's certainly articulate enough. And I know he won't slant the discussion toward either his country or ours. But all that aside, we don't really have a choice. They could easily just cancel the whole thing."

"They wouldn't."

"They would. They've done things like that in the past."

Ginny shook her head. "What else can they do to us?"

"I don't even want to think about it. How's our video equipment coming?"

"I was just talking to Doug. He's nearly set up."

"Is there any way to tell if customs tampered with the camera the way they did with your dryer?"

"Doug said that the seals he attached to them before we left the States were unbroken."

"Good news at last. They should still be working. At least that's one thing we don't have to worry about."

Ginny briskly rubbed her arms. "I don't believe how cold it is in here."

"Do you want to borrow one of my sweaters? I brought a suitcase full of them."

"I might take you up on that a little later. Right now I've got some other details to check."

"Have you had any luck locating a horseshoe-shaped table?"

"Not yet."

"Keep trying. I've told them for months how important that particular kind of table is."

"If I have to take a round one and saw a horseshoe out of it, we'll have one."

The rest of the day was hectic as both the American and Soviet crews got ready. Sound levels had to be set; lighting had to be fixed and backdrops made attractive for television. By the time evening rolled around and they had to get ready for the cocktail party, both Kendall and Ginny were dragging. They met at the elevator, looked silently at each other with tired eyes, and leaned against the walls as they rode to the fifth floor. The concierge politely tipped his hat at them.

Ginny sighed as they walked down the hall. "I don't know about you, but I'd just as soon have room service and go to bed early. I still haven't recovered from the trip over here."

"I know, but it's a nice gesture on their part. We'll have fun once we get there."

"I've heard that before."

Kendall laughed as she left Ginny at her door and walked on to her own room. Taking from her drawer the small bottle of bubble bath she'd brought from home, she started a hot bath and poured in a generous amount. It foamed up invitingly and Kendall, still cold, gingerly stripped and stepped into a little bit of heaven.

She could have spent the night there, and in fact did stay longer than she should have, sliding down into the tub and leaning her head against the back of it, running more hot water as soon as it began to cool even a little.

For the first time that day, her thoughts had a chance to drift, and they went straight to Alexei. If he was going to be the new moderator, she was going to be seeing him again. But as much as she wanted that, she knew as well as Alexei that it was a double-edged sword. The more she was with him, the more deeply ingrained he became in her heart. Kendall couldn't help but wonder why he'd accepted the job as moderator.

With a shake of her head to clear her thoughts, Kendall climbed out of the bathtub and dried herself off, then wrapped herself in the thick terry robe she'd had the foresight to pack while she examined the contents of her closet. She'd brought two dresses that would be appropriate for tonight. One was a rich purple taffeta that left her arms and shoulders bare, fitted her figure closely to just below her hips and then flared out into three tiers of material that reached just below her knees. The other consisted of two pieces; the top was a black velvet bustier that formed a V just below her waist and the full, feminine skirt was bright red taffeta that was the same length as the other dress. In the end, the black velvet won because it was unquestionably warmer. She'd had no idea the hotel was going to be so cold. If she had, she would have brought more functional cocktail dresses.

With regretful hesitation, she removed the soft warmth of her robe and dressed. Her makeup and hair, which she left loose, only took a few minutes.

Taking no purse, but pocketing her room key in her skirt, Kendall left her room and knocked on Ginny's door.

"Coming!"

The room behind her was the picture of chaos with clothes strewn everywhere, when Ginny opened the door, wearing a navy blue and white polka dot cocktail dress with a flower at her waist. She eyed Kendall's outfit. "Red?" she asked dryly.

"I know it's tempting fate, but . . ." Kendall lifted her shoulders expressively.

"I'll say. I've always liked that outfit, though." She closed her door behind her and they headed down the hall. As before, the concierge tipped his hat at them.

"Did you see how bleary his eyes are?" Ginny whispered to Kendall as they waited for the elevator. "I wonder if his hat is the only thing he's been tipping."

A laugh escaped before Kendall could catch it. The concierge looked at the two women struggling for composure for a moment and then went back to his magazine.

After they got on the elevator and the doors had blissfully closed, Ginny rolled her eyes. "This is awful. I feel like I'm back in boarding school."

"It is a little like that, isn't it?"

"A little? That's exactly the way it is. We're adults and they watch us like children."

"Different country, different customs."

"All I know is that I've been here for one day and I'm ready to go home. What about you?"

"Not at all. I want to at least see Moscow before we have to leave."

"I wish I was more curious. Did you notice what a depressingly gray day it was?"

"I read something that said between October and March, Moscow averages only about fifteen minutes of sunshine a day."

"That's horrible. Maybe that's why drinking is such a problem here."

"I wouldn't doubt it."

As soon as Kendall and Ginny got to the lobby, they were shown to what must once have been the hotel ballroom. Huge chandeliers hung from the elaborately plastered ceiling. Scrolled pillars circled the room, some of them in desperate need of a fresh coat of paint. Though Kendall didn't see any musicians, an intense Rachmaninoff piano concerto played in the background.

"Would you look at the food!" Ginny whispered.

Huge banquet tables sagged under the weight of mountains of food.

The people present, approximately five hundred, didn't fill the room by any means, but made for a comfortable gathering. Kendall spotted members of her group speaking animatedly with their Soviet counterparts—sometimes with the benefit of translators and sometimes without. But everyone seemed to be understanding everyone else and more importantly, having a good time.

"Miss Stuart?" said a thickly accented voice behind her.

Kendall turned to find a man about six feet tall with thinning brown hair and a cruel mouth standing there. "Yes?"

He extended his hand and executed a sharp bow when Kendall placed hers in it. "I am Boris Breskov. I saw you from afar when I was working in your country."

He didn't look at all familiar to her. "When were you there?" she asked politely.

"For a few years, until last summer."

"That's a coincidence. I know someone else who left about then. Alexei Demyenov. Have you ever met him?"

"Yes, I believe so." He smiled at her and Kendall literally recoiled. This man emanated cruelty. She wanted to get away from him but couldn't think of a way to make a gracious exit without her distaste becoming obvious.

A hand touched her elbow. "Kendall, there's someone I'd like you to meet."

She looked up gratefully into Alexei's eyes. "Of course. Excuse me, please, Mr. Breskov."

He turned his attention to Alexei now and his smile grew even more threatening. "Oh, please, don't take her away so soon. We were just getting to know one another."

"I'm sorry," Kendall apologized. "I've forgotten my manners. Alexei Demyenov, this is Boris . . ."

"Breskov," the man supplied for her as he extended his hand toward Alexei.

Alexei seemed not to notice the hand. "We've met," he said shortly.

Boris's hand fell to his side. His lips thinned.

Kendall sensed the strain but didn't know what to do about it. "We were just discussing the fact that you two were in America at about the same time."

"Isn't that interesting?" the agent asked, seeming to enjoy himself.

"Fascinating." Alexei's tone was abrupt. He wasn't even trying to be polite.

Kendall looked at Alexei in surprise.

"I hope," the agent said as he took her hand in both of his, "that you and I will have a chance to get to know each other better during the time you're here. Perhaps we could have dinner..."

"Oh, I don't think so," she demurred with a charming smile. No one could possibly have taken offense. "My days and nights are so occupied with this conference that I don't really have any time for myself."

"That's a pity. You should make time. I'd like the chance to show you Moscow."

"Perhaps another visit."

He bowed low over her hand. "I'll certainly look forward to just such an occasion."

Alexei put his hand possessively at her waist and moved her out of Boris Breskov's range.

"Thank you," she whispered as soon as she and Alexei were out of earshot.

"Stay away from that man," he said firmly.

"I intend to. He gives me the creeps. Who is he?"

"KGB."

Somehow she wasn't surprised. "Is that why he left America at the same time you did?"

"He's my shadow. Every move I make, he makes. Every thought I have, he wants to know about."

"Why? What's the point?"

"Supposedly to make sure I don't do anything I'm not supposed to."

"Supposedly?"

"Let's just say that he takes his duties a few steps further than that." Alexei looked down at her and a corner of his mouth turned up even as his brown eyes softened. "You look beautiful."

His look and words warmed her. She gazed from his conservative dark suit to his eyes. "So do you."

His smile grew.

"I heard you're going to be our moderator starting tomorrow."

"That's what I'm told."

"What you're told? You mean you didn't volunteer?"

"Hardly. I was in the middle of preparations to leave Moscow."

"To leave?" Kendall asked curiously. "For another assignment?"

Alexei said nothing and suddenly she understood.

"Oh." There was a world of pain in that one word. "To get away from me."

"As far away as I could."

Kendall's eyes dropped, but Alexei reached out a gentle hand and raised her face to his. "Seeing you but not being able to have you is a pain I find almost beyond bearing."

"But you *can* have me," she said softly. "You've chosen not to."

"There's been very little choice in anything I've done regarding you."

"Whether you like it or not, you and I are going to be together almost constantly for the next ten days. Instead of fighting what's between us, why can't we give in to it for that time?"

Alexei's eyes roamed over her lovely face. "I wish I could allow myself that freedom."

"The only one keeping you from it is you. The only one keeping you from me is you."

"It's much more complicated than you understand, Kendall."

"Then explain it to me. Make me understand."

"Somehow I think that would only make it worse."

"How could anything be worse than this?"

Boris Breskov stood not ten feet away, a plate laden with food in his hands, and watched the scene being played out between Alexei and Kendall. It was easy for him to see why Alexei found her so appealing. In fact, he was rather amazed at the other man's resolve to stay away from her. But now she was here and he'd neatly arranged for them to have continual contact. This, he had a feeling, was going to be the straw that broke the camel's back. This time he was going to show that Alexei Demyenov had the feet of clay he'd recognized all along. Maybe after that the man would give him a little respect.

Alexei spotted the KGB agent watching. "Let's just talk about business, Kendall."

The ache inside her grew. "All right." She forced herself to concentrate. "I'd like you to meet with the moderator we brought with us and find out what he intended to do so that you know what the structure is going to be."

"Where is he?"

Her eyes roamed over the different faces in the room until she found one with a short blond beard. "There he is. His name is Ted Shields."

"Does he know that he's been replaced?"

"I told him this afternoon. He wasn't thrilled, but he understands that there's nothing we can do about it. You aren't the villain in the piece."

She walked with Alexei to where Ted was standing and introduced the two men. Ted was gracious, as she'd known he would be, and within minutes they were immersed in work. Kendall listened for a time, punctuating their conversation with her thoughts, but then realized they were handling everything just fine on their own. Without saying anything to distract them, Kendall drifted away.

Alexei watched her go.

Ted saw the look and touched Alexei's arm in a friendly fashion. "I know she's a knockout, but don't even bother putting a move on her. You'd be doing nothing but wasting your time."

Alexei's eyes were still on her as she moved through the people making polite conversation. "I can't imagine that doing anything with her would be a waste of time."

"Trust me on this. There are women who can be had and women who can't be. She's a definite can't-be."

Alexei smiled without amusement at the irony of the words. "I'll remember that."

"Now, where were we?"

Kendall stopped here and there, trying to put on a cheerful face. She was amazed by how many Soviets spoke English. Some of it was difficult to understand, but it was English.

Ginny materialized by her side. "I saw you talking to Alexei. Anything interesting?"

"What do you mean by interesting?"

"Are you two getting together?"

"He doesn't want to."

Ginny shook her head. "I don't understand."

"Join the club. I all but offered myself to him and he turned me down."

Ginny squeezed her friend's hand. "You're really upset, aren't you?"

"You bet I am. I love him. We have ten days when we could be together—ten days together that we could take away with us and treasure as memories when we have nothing else left—and he just won't."

"He must have his reasons."

"I'm sure he does." Kendall sighed and shook her head. "Oh, Ginny, of all the men in the world, why do you suppose I had to fall in love with one I can't have?"

"Fate."

"It's frightening, this power he has over me. And it's frightening because I know, deep in my soul, that I'm never going to feel this way about another human being. It's almost as though he's a part of me and always has been. I just didn't realize it until I met him."

"I've seen the way Alexei looks at you, Kendall. Whatever you may think, he does have some feelings for you."

"I know. But somehow he's able to distance himself from them in a way I just can't."

"Maybe. Maybe not. It could be that he's simply trying to make the best of a bad situation."

"Being with me for what little time we have would be making the best of a bad situation."

Ginny caught Alexei watching them and was startled by the depth of pain she saw in his eyes. "Perhaps he's just handling the pain the best way he knows how," she suggested quietly.

Kendall sighed and looked around. "It was nice of the Soviets to do this," she said, neatly changing the subject, "but I hope it doesn't last too much longer. I'm so tired I can barely stand."

"Somehow this group doesn't strike me as a partying crowd. I bet we'll be in bed before midnight."

"Let's keep our fingers crossed. In the meantime, I suppose we should mingle."

"One of my favorite things."

"How is our group doing?"

"They're a little nervous about tomorrow, but otherwise having a good time."

"I've been watching them with the Soviets. They seem to be striking up some friendships."

"I noticed that, too. I think basically these people like westerners. I wasn't expecting that kind of reaction."

Kendall agreed.

"Well, I'm off." As Ginny walked past Kendall, she beamed her smile at someone and said out of the corner of her mouth. "Mingle, mingle, mingle."

Ginny had been right about the party not lasting until midnight. By eleven-thirty, Kendall was in her dark room, wrapped in her robe and sitting on the window seat looking out at the cold, white world beyond. She wished she could picture where Alexei was so she could have something to hold on to. For all that

Kendall felt she knew what kind of man he was, there was still an element of mystery to him. Did anyone really know Alexei Demyenov?

Alexei sat in the living room of the dacha, or country house, he'd purchased not long after returning from America. A fire crackled in the fireplace and shadows of the flames danced on the walls. He picked up a worn book. It automatically fell open. He took out the dry white rose and gazed at it in the firelight, then leaned his head against the back of his couch and stared at nothing in particular while still holding the rose.

Chapter Eight

Kendall was so deeply engrossed in the notes she was making that when someone lightly touched her shoulder, she jumped and gasped. "Oh, Ginny," she said as she put her hand over her pounding heart. "Don't sneak up on me like that."

"Sorry, but you didn't answer when I said your name. What are you writing?"

"Just some points I want to make sure get covered by Alexei in the last hour of today's conference."

Ginny sat in the chair behind Kendall and looked around the bustling room. Technicians were getting their cameras and sound equipment ready. The Americans and Soviets were starting to take their seats. "I can't believe this is the last day."

"We still have a weekend left," Kendall said as she continued writing.

"I meant the last working day. How do you think it went?"

"Beautifully. Alexei's been incredible."

"He really has," Ginny agreed. "He's been walking a tightrope between his side and ours, but you'd never know it to watch him. He seems so relaxed."

"Relaxed, but his mind is always working." Kendall had been watching him work for ten days and found herself in awe of the extent of his knowledge and his ability to apply it to what they were doing without hitting anyone over the head with it.

"You've held up rather well," Ginny told her admiringly.

Kendall stopped writing and looked at her friend. "It hasn't been easy. Every day when I leave my room I have to remind myself that I'm a professional."

"Well, however you've done it, it's worked. I know it's been tough, though. You must be relieved that it's almost over."

"I don't know," Kendall said softly. "In a way I am. And in another way I'm starting to feel a little lost."

As she was talking to Ginny, Kendall spotted Alexei walking across the room.

Ginny followed her gaze. Even her heart pounded a little harder at the sight of him, so tall and dark. She could imagine how Kendall must feel. "Well, I'll leave you to it."

"Where are you going?"

"To have some breakfast. I'm starving."

"Would you bring me back some tea?"

"Sure. See you later."

Taking a deep breath and once more reminding herself that she was a professional, Kendall took her notes to the front of the room where Alexei was standing talking to one of the American panelists.

"Excuse me," she said politely.

Alexei turned to her and smiled when he saw that her hair was pulled back into a ponytail. It went with her jeans and oversize pale pink sweater.

"What are you smiling at?" she asked.

"You. I like you like this."

Kendall looked down at herself, then back at him. "Thank you."

He inclined his dark head toward her notepad. "Is there something you wanted to discuss with me?"

"Oh!" She didn't know how, but she'd almost forgotten. "I've been making some notes about things I want to make sure get covered in the final session today."

Alexei moved behind Kendall and read over her shoulder. Kendall could feel the heat of his body through her sweater, even though he wasn't touching her. And he smelled wonderful. Exactly the way she remembered. She closed her eyes for a moment and took a deep breath, little knowing that Alexei was thinking the same things about her.

"What's this one?" he said pointing to something she'd written rather quickly and illegibly.

"Oh. In my preparation for this I came across some interesting items, and this one in particular I'd like you to ask the Soviets about. According to Karl Marx, the State is an instrument of oppression. He dreamed of a society in which workers and peasants would manage their own factories and land and the State would simply wither away.''

''That's true.''

''And yet here the State is all-powerful.''

''That's also true.''

''I just thought that might be an interesting point to make.''

''Consider it done. And do you also want me to ask the Americans about what a true democracy means?''

Kendall looked at him over her shoulder and smiled. ''I had a feeling you'd get me on that one.''

Alexei looked into her eyes. He'd kept his distance for ten days and he couldn't do it any longer. He needed to be with her. ''Come out with me this afternoon.''

That was the last thing she expected to hear. ''What?''

''You've spent your entire time here locked away in this hotel. It's criminal. When we've finished today, come with me and let me show you Moscow.''

''Are you sure you want to do that?'' she asked quietly.

''I'm sure.'' There was no doubt in his voice. No hesitation at all.

Kendall looked into his eyes a moment longer. ''All right. I'd like that.''

''And wear exactly what you have on. We're going to be doing a lot of walking.'' Taking her notepad, he walked away from her toward his working area.

''That looked friendly,'' Ginny said as she handed Kendall a cup of tea.

"It was," Kendall admitted, bemusement evident in her voice. Then looking at her friend as though realizing that Ginny shouldn't be there, she frowned. "I thought you were going to have breakfast."

"Too late. They stopped serving five minutes before I walked into the restaurant."

"I have some cookies in my room that I kept from the airplane. You're welcome to them."

"Believe me, if I get desperate enough, I just might take you up on it."

Kendall sipped the hot tea and sighed. "Thanks. This is wonderful."

"What time do you think we'll be finished today?"

"One o'clock."

"Good."

"Why good?"

"Because I have a date."

"With whom?"

Ginny smiled and waved at one of the Soviet panelists. "Isn't he lovely?"

"Only if you like blond-haired, blue-eyed Adonises."

"I do, I do." She looked at Kendall. "What are you doing with your afternoon?"

"Apparently I'm spending it with Alexei."

"You're kidding."

"He just asked me."

"Are you sure that's a wise thing for you to do?"

"No. I'm not sure at all. I just know I want to be with him, even if it's only for a few hours."

Half an hour later the last segment of the conference was under way. Kendall quietly took a seat and watched with the same intensity that she had for the past ten days. Alexei moved easily within the horseshoe opening of the table that Ginny had finally managed to locate. Sometimes he'd lean casually against a corner of the table, his long legs stretched out in front of him, while listening intently to someone speak. He paced as he talked. He rarely left any kind of broad statement unchallenged by either side, and would turn suddenly to one of the panelists, call him or her by name and say, "What do you think about that?" Once they told him, he dug even more deeply, tossing it back and forth between the panelists like a hot potato that no one wanted to hold for very long. In short, he was magnificent, and Kendall's respect for him grew even greater.

As soon as the final words had been spoken, a round of applause went up from the panelists. Kendall, beaming, clapped, too. They had all been wonderful. Alexei shook everyone's hand and Kendall followed not far behind him. As worried as she'd been about the outcome, she was now as proud of this as anything she'd done.

"All right," she said standing in the middle of the group. "How many of you are planning to go on that bus tour around the city this afternoon?"

All of the Americans answered in the affirmative.

"It's leaving in fifteen minutes so you'd better get your coats and whatever else you're going to need."

As everyone headed for the elevators, Alexei walked to Kendall. "Are you ready to go?"

"I have to get my..."

"Here you go," Ginny said as she handed Kendall her coat, scarf and gloves. "I thought you might be needing these, so I figured while I was upstairs getting my stuff I might as well get yours, too."

"Thank you."

Alexei helped Kendall into her coat, and while she was buttoning it, he draped her wool scarf over her head and shoulders. "I know it's warmer today than it has been, but you still have to take care not to get a chill." He picked up his own coat from the back of a chair and put it on as they walked out the door. "What would you like to see first?"

"I don't know. I suppose St. Basil's Cathedral."

His eyes smiled at her. "A woman who knows her monuments."

"Everyone knows that building with its colorful onion domes. It seems like every time you see a picture of Moscow, St. Basil's is hovering in the background."

Alexei took her gloved hand in his and the two of them strolled companionably in the afternoon light toward Red Square. They passed through several parks. Old men wrapped snugly in their coats played chess. Even older men attended penny scales where people stopped to weigh themselves. Women pushed baby carriages on runners instead of wheels over the snow-covered ground. Ice skaters glided over frozen ponds to music piped out to them. Kendall was charmed. "I've never seen so many parks in one city."

"Moscow is forty percent parks."

Near the subway, men and women wearing placards filled with Cyrillic lettering spoke animatedly to
the crowds around them. "What's going on there?"
she asked.

"A housing exchange."

"A what?"

"Here, once a citizen obtains an apartment from the
government, it becomes like a small fiefdom that can
be traded, rented or even bequeathed to children. They
come here with the specifics of their apartments written on those placards and do the best they can to make
good trades."

On they walked until suddenly there it was before
them. St. Basil's was a much more stunning vision in
reality than it ever was in a picture. Kendall stopped
and just looked.

"It's a combination of nine churches," Alexei explained. "There is the central structure surrounded by
those eight domed chapels. Each of the chapels honor
saints on whose days Ivan the Terrible won battles
against the Tartars."

"Is there anything you don't know?" she asked with
a smile.

"Not about Russian history."

Still holding hands, they went through Red Square,
past Lenin's tomb and the GUM department store.
Kendall marveled at the line that snaked around the
outside of the store. It went on for blocks. "I wonder
what they're waiting for?"

"I'll ask." Alexei stopped next to a woman at the
end of the line and spoke to her in Russian. She an-

swered in a rapid-fire spate. Alexei thanked her and
started walking with Kendall again.

"Well?"

"She doesn't know."

Kendall stopped and faced him. "She's standing in
line and she doesn't know why?"

"You have to understand that women in Moscow
stand in line an average of fourteen hours a week."

"Do they usually know why?"

Alexei tweaked her nose. "Yes, my pretty. But today, when she was walking past GUM and saw all the
people, she decided something special must be on sale
and she can't get in to see what it is unless she stands
in line."

"Ah. Why are there so many lines?"

"Several reasons," Alexei explained as they started
walking again. "Chronic shortages of many basics
that Americans take for granted. You can't just go
shopping on a whim. You must go when the product
is available. And then there's employment."

"Employment?"

"Everyone has a right to a job, but sometimes to
live up to that, jobs must be created. Let's say you
want to buy a pound of cheese. You go to the store and
wait in one line to pick out the cheese from one clerk.
Then you wait in a second line to pay another clerk for
the cheese and then you stand in a third line to show
your receipt and pick up your cheese from yet another clerk. Three people doing the job of one."

"I guess every country has its own way of doing
things."

"A very bland comment."

"I've learned the hard way not to criticize the way others do things. Where are we going now?"

"I have some friends I'd like you to meet."

The sun was beginning to set and the air was getting chillier as they went into an old section of Moscow not far from Kendall's hotel. Walking into what must once have been a beautiful home but was now divided into several apartments, they went up bare, creaking steps to the second floor. A woman in her early thirties answered Alexei's knock. Her eyes lit up at the sight of him. "Alexei!" She said something in Russian, but when prompted by Alexei, spoke in English. "You didn't tell us you were coming." She hugged him and then turned to Kendall and hugged her, too. "And you must be the American we've heard so much about. I'm Anna and this," she said, indicating a handsome man a few years older than herself, "is my husband Nikolai."

Nikolai gave Kendall a friendly smile and a handshake, then hugged Alexei. "Welcome. Can you stay for dinner?" he asked as he took their coats and hung them in an already crowded closet.

"If you have enough," Alexei accepted. "It wasn't our intention to intrude on your meal."

"It's not an intrusion. Please—" Anna took Kendall's arm and led her to the couch, "—sit."

This seemed to be the only room, aside from a small kitchen hidden behind curtains, from which wonderful aromas were emanating, and a bathroom off to the side.

"You got the new couch, I see," Alexei said.

Anna looked at it and sighed. "Yes."

"What's wrong?"

"When I die, no one will know what kind of taste I had. All my life I have bought what is available and not what I wanted. But," she lifted her hands, "such is life. And on that melancholy note, please excuse me, but I have food cooking."

"Do you need some help?"

"Not at all. You stay and talk. I won't be long."

Nikolai filled a pipe with tobacco and lit it. "We've been watching your program on television," he told Kendall. "It was enlightening."

"That was in large measure due to the way Alexei handled the panelists."

"So he would have you believe," Nikolai said with a laugh.

Anna came out of the kitchen and cleared off what looked to be a work table, extended it and topped it with a white tablecloth.

"How much longer are you going to be in Moscow?" Anna asked as she worked.

"We leave for home tomorrow morning."

"That's not very long."

"I know."

"Have you had a chance to see the city at all?"

"Today's the first time."

Anna looked at Nikolai and said something in Russian. He nodded agreement. "We have some tickets to a poetry reading by Valeria Minov tonight. You and Alexei must take them."

"Oh, no, we couldn't," Kendall tried to decline.

"Please. It's an experience you should have. We can go another time."

Kendall looked helplessly at Alexei. "That's very generous of you and Nikolai, Anna. We accept with gratitude."

Kendall was amazed at the generosity of these people who seemed to have so little.

"You'll have to eat fast if you're going to make it on time." Anna quickly put the food on the table and everyone sat down. There was a wonderful clear soup, two kinds of bread, potatoes drenched in butter, duck in gravy and fried cheese cakes with plum jam, iced vodka and a thick, sweet tea. It was a dietitian's nightmare—and absolutely delicious. Kendall savored every bite.

Dinner conversation was energetic between their two hosts, but Alexei was strangely quiet. Her eyes met his across the table and held. "What do you think about that?" Nikolai suddenly asked her.

Kendall tore her eyes from Alexei's. "I'm sorry. What do I think about what?"

He smiled and patted her shoulder. "Never mind. Your thoughts are obviously elsewhere."

"Oh, no," Anna said as she looked at her watch. "It's late. You've no time for dessert."

Kendall looked down at her jeans and sweater. "I can't go like this."

"You look fine," Alexei assured her as he accepted her coat from Nikolai and helped her into it. "People wear whatever they want to these readings."

"Are you sure?"

"Positive."

Still uncertain, she hugged Anna. "The food was delicious. I'm sorry to run out on you without helping with the dishes."

"I wouldn't have let you help under any circumstances," Anna said with a smile. "Please, enjoy yourselves."

The last Kendall saw of them, Anna and Nikolai were standing in the doorway waving, their arms around each other. "You have nice friends," she told Alexei.

"Yes," he agreed. "Now you do, too." They waited for some light traffic to pass, then crossed the street. "I have to get my car so we can drive to the concert hall. It's not far from here."

"Concert hall?" she asked in surprise as she lengthened her stride to keep up with him.

"What were you expecting?"

"Oh, I don't know. A little supper club, I suppose."

Alexei's teeth flashed white in his handsome face. "Oh, Kendall, are you in for a surprise."

Was she ever. Parking around the brightly lit hall was impossible. They ended up blocks away, walking behind a whole throng of people all going to the same place. The hall itself was elaborately decorated with low-hanging chandeliers running the length of the stage. Vases of red and white carnations dotted the area between the stage and the audience. The nearly two thousand seats were covered in a plush red material—and both the women and the men were very dressed up.

Kendall looked at Alexei as they made their way down the aisle to their seats. "People wear pretty much anything they want, do they?"

He grinned down at her. "Would you have come if I'd told you the truth?"

"No."

"Then the end justifies the means. Keep your coat on if you're uncomfortable."

When they were settled into their seats, Kendall watched in amazement as the rest of the hall filled to capacity. "All of this for a poetry reading?"

"In Moscow, the only thing more popular than a poetry reading is a soccer match."

"I had no idea."

"We Russians all have the souls of poets."

The lights blinked and a hush fell over the crowd. As the lights over the audience dimmed, the chandeliers onstage sparkled to brilliant life. A small woman with dark brown hair, dressed in black pants and sweater, spiked heels on her feet, approached the lonely microphone. There was nothing else on stage. No one applauded. If anything, the silence became more intense.

As the woman began to speak in a strong, expressive voice, Alexei leaned toward Kendall, his mouth near her ear, translating the words. She recited her work for over an hour, moving some of the people in the audience to tears with the power of her words. But it was the final poem that affected Kendall the most:

I turn away and try to leave.
You catch my hand and bid me stay.
Our eyes meet;
Our lips touch;

Our bodies join together, bittersweet, one last
time.

It was fate that brought us together, my darling,
And fate is tearing us apart,
Leaving us stranded helplessly in its wake.

I ache as I leave you
Knowing I'll never be whole again until you're in
my arms.
I ache as I leave you
Knowing in my heart that this is the end.

But I cannot regret the time that we've shared.
I cannot regret loving you.
And if fate should decree that our eyes never meet
again,
Knowing you—loving you—is worth the pain.
And even though we'll be world's apart,
I will carry you always in my heart.

Alexei's breath was warm against Kendall's ear as
he finished translating the words for her. Kendall
turned her head and looked into his eyes. Her own
were swimming. He leaned over and kissed the cor-
ners of her mouth, but offered no comforting words.
A moment later, as Valeria Minov left the stage and
the house lights came up, uproarious applause
erupted. Kendall expected her to come back and take
a bow, but she didn't. Once she was gone, she was
gone.

Kendall was very quiet as they left the building and
walked to his car. As Alexei started to open the door
for her, Kendall put her hand over his. "I want to go
somewhere where we can be alone together. Please."

"Kendall . . ."

"I need to be with you."

Alexei looked into her eyes and was lost. Without saying anything else, he helped her into the car, drove to the Moscow River and parked. He got out and walked around to open her door, then with her hand in his, took her to a waiting troika that was sitting on the thick ice. Alexei gave Kendall a hand up into the back and spoke to the driver in Russian as he settled in next to her and tucked the heavy blankets around them for warmth.

The man spoke softly to his horse and with a musical jingle, the muscular animal began pulling them easily across the ice, avoiding the men who sat on upended buckets with fishing lines dangling through holes they'd drilled in the solid surface.

Kendall didn't ask any questions. She just moved closer to Alexei. He wrapped his arm around her shoulders and held her close to his side.

After forty-five minutes, Alexei said something to the driver and they slowed down. The next time Alexei spoke, they stopped completely. He handed the man some money and got out of the troika, then lifted Kendall out. As the music of the sleigh bells disappeared into the distance, Alexei and Kendall climbed snow-laden stairs to a dark home. Alexei opened the door with a key and turned on a light. It was so cold inside that Kendall could see her breath.

"Whose is this?" Kendall asked as she looked around.

"Mine."

"I thought you lived in Moscow."

"I have an apartment there. But after being in your home, I realized I wanted a place where I could truly be alone when I felt the need. I bought this."

It was small with only four rooms, but comfortable and inviting. While Kendall wandered through, Alexei built a fire in the fireplace, tending it until the flames licked their way around the wood and lent an orange glow to the room.

Kendall turned out the light and kneeled next to him on the thick scatter rug.

"Kendall . . ." Alexei began.

She put one hand on his shoulder and shook her head as she touched her fingers lightly to his mouth.

The fire crackling and hissing was the only noise except for the steady beat of their hearts.

Kendall, still on her knees, moved even closer until their bodies touched. She raised her hand to his thick, dark hair. "I know you think you should protect me," she said softly, "but I'm not a child. I don't need your protection, Alexei. I need you."

With a soft groan, his mouth came down on hers, unleashing a torrent of passion that had been building within him for months. Their coats slid unnoticed to the floor. Alexei lowered her onto the rug, his mouth never leaving hers.

Kendall reached up under his sweater and ran her fingers over his smoothly muscled back, pulling him closer to her.

He trailed his mouth over the clean line of her jaw as his hand moved under her sweater and across her velvet skin.

She arched against him and Alexei moaned again. But it was as though that sound brought him to his senses. He pushed himself away from her and got to his feet. "No," he said as he dragged a shaky hand through his hair. "We can't do this. I promised myself I wouldn't make love to you unless you were my wife."

Kendall sat up. "Then make me your wife."

"I've tried to tell you . . ."

"I know. And I've tried to understand. I know things are going to be difficult for us, but we can find a way to be together. We have to, Alexei. Can't you see how much we belong with each other?"

Alexei walked back to Kendall and kneeled in front of her, his expression softening as he looked into her gray eyes. "I know. I've known it since the day we met."

"I love you so much."

He trailed the back of his hand down her smooth cheek. "You mean more to me than my life."

"Then at least let us have tonight together. And if you won't have me without marriage, then marry me."

"And if we never see each other again? What happens to you?"

"Don't you understand, Alexei? It doesn't matter. I could never be married to anyone else."

Alexei leaned over and kissed her warmly. "Will you marry me, Kendall?"

A tremulous smile touched her lovely mouth. "Yes," she said softly.

He shook his head. "Oh, Kendall. I hope you know what you're doing. You could find yourself married to a man you'll never see again after tomorrow."

"That's a risk I'm willing to take."

He pulled her to him and gave her a slow, deep kiss. "All right," he said softly as he looked into her eyes. "I have some calls to make first."

Chapter Nine

Kendall sat still, lost in her thoughts, unaware of the passage of time until she heard someone enter the house. A moment later Nikolai and Anna stood in the doorway.

Kendall rose and smiled, genuinely glad to see them. "You must be the phone call that Alexei made."

"One of them," Anna said. "Niki, turn on a light."

He flipped a switch above the couch and Kendall saw for the first time that Anna was carrying a large box which she now put on a chair and opened. From inside, she lifted out a stunning creamy satin and lace wedding dress. "This belonged to my grandmother. After her, my mother wore it and after my mother, I wore it. Now, if you will, I'd like you to."

Kendall didn't know what to say to that kind of generosity. "Thank you," she finally managed, simply and with all her heart. "It's beautiful."

Anna hugged her. "We haven't known each other long, but if Alexei loves you, how can we do less?"

Alexei walked in at that moment and stood with his arms around Kendall. "Good. You made it. We have to be at the church in fifteen minutes."

"Church?"

He looked down at Kendall. "We won't have the sanction of the state, but we're going to have a real church wedding."

Anna took Kendall's hand and led her from the room. "We'd better get you ready."

And get her ready they did. While Kendall took her hair out of the ponytail and combed it until it shone, Anna worked on the dress. They slipped it over Kendall's head and Anna patiently buttoned her into it. "It's a little large in the waist," she remarked, "but other than that, perfect." She stepped away. "Now turn around and let me look at you."

Kendall obediently turned and Anna beamed at her. "Wait until Alexei sees you!" She moved closer to Kendall and lightly pinched her cheeks. "You're almost as pale as the dress. Do you have any makeup?" Anna asked.

Kendall shook her head. "I didn't even bring a purse with me."

Anna fished through her own purse and came up with a lipstick. "Here. This will add some color."

Kendall's hand was shaking as she raised it to her mouth, but she managed to get it on straight.

Anna looked at her again. "There. That's all you need." With her hands on Kendall's shoulders, Anna turned her toward the mirror. "Look at yourself."

Kendall did. In the dim light of the bedroom lamp, she looked like a princess in a fairy tale.

"Now, we go."

When the women walked into the living room, the men rose. Alexei's dark eyes moved over Kendall with exquisite slowness. He walked to her and tilted her face to his. "You look beautiful," he said in a low voice meant only for her ears, and kissed her tenderly. When he raised his head, he gazed into her eyes. "It's not too late to back out of this."

Kendall shook her head. "I want to be your wife."

After a moment, as though he had a debate with himself, Alexei picked up Kendall's coat and draped it over her shoulders. Anna and Nikolai wordlessly led the way to their car. The drive to the small church over the snow-encrusted streets took only a few minutes.

No one noticed the other car as it moved slowly behind them, its headlights off.

When they arrived, a priest dressed in black robes and headpiece that hadn't changed in design for centuries greeted them at the door. His thick, well-tended gray beard reached to the middle of his barrel chest. He spoke in Russian to Alexei and in English to Kendall. In the church behind him, dozens of candles flickered, but there were no electric lights.

Anna took their coats while Nikolai closed the doors. "The Russian Orthodox ceremony is broken into three parts," Alexei explained gently as he took Kendall's hand in his. "The first, the betrothal, or the exchange of rings, takes place here. The second, the crowning, takes place in the middle of the church. The third, or the uncrowning, takes place in the front of the church. Are you nervous?''

Kendall met Alexei's look with a direct one of her own. She'd never been more sure of anything in her life. "No."

His dark eyes smiled.

"I don't have a ring for you, though," she said.

"That's all right."

The priest returned at that moment carrying two candles. He handed one to Kendall and one to Alexei and then began speaking in Russian as he looked from one to the other of them like a benevolent father. Alexei handed his candle to Nikolai who stood just to his right, then picked up Kendall's trembling left hand in his and slipped on a carved gold band. He squeezed her hand reassuringly before taking his candle back.

They then went to the middle of the church. As the priest spoke, Anna placed a crown on Kendall's head while Nikolai did the same to Alexei.

Again they followed the priest to the front of the old church where the two of them drank wine from the same goblet. Anna and Nikolai removed the crowns. Alexei took Kendall's right hand in his and the priest looped a cloth around their joined hands, then led them three times in a circle, the most perfect form, before untying them. Covering their hands with his, he spoke in English. "Go into the world and be happy with each other. Love unto death."

Forty minutes after they'd walked into the country church, Kendall and Alexei became man and wife. Alexei cupped Kendall's face in his hands and looked for a long time into her eyes before kissing her.

The four of them signed their names into the church's register and then in silence drove to Alexei's cottage. As Kendall and Alexei got out of the car, Anna kissed first Kendall and then Alexei on both cheeks. "Take care of yourselves."

Alexei wrapped his arm around Kendall. "We'll be fine."

Anna didn't look convinced.

"If you need anything, call," said Nikolai.

Kendall and Alexei watched them drive away, then climbed the steps into the cottage. The fire was still burning. Alexei took Kendall's coat from her shoulders and then his own black suit coat. Without saying anything, he put another log on the fire and turned to his wife. "Come here."

Kendall stood in front of him.

He raised his hand and ran his fingers reverently through her silky hair. "I love you so much."

She caught his hand in hers and kissed his palm, then raised her eyes to his.

Alexei was stunned by the depth of feeling he saw. He lowered his mouth to hers and felt her lips part softly, invitingly beneath his. With exquisite slowness, he explored the inner reaches of her mouth, getting to know the taste of her, this woman he loved beyond reason.

He walked around behind Kendall and swept her hair away from the back of her neck and over her shoulder. With skilled fingers, he began undoing the tiny pearl buttons that went all the way to her waist. There must have been fifty of them. As he worked his way down her back, Alexei's mouth followed his fingers. When he got to the last button, kneeling behind her, he put both hands at her waist and kissed her at the base of her spine.

As he rose, he trailed his hands up her sides and over her shoulders, sliding the gown from first one shoulder and then the other until it fell from her completely and landed in a satiny circle at her feet.

Still behind Kendall, Alexei wrapped his arm around her waist and pulled her body against his. His warm mouth kissed the side of her neck.

Kendall raised her arm and reached behind her to tangle her fingers in his thick hair.

Alexei's hands slid down over her. He turned Kendall in his arms. "We only have tonight," he said in a voice husky with desire.

Kendall loosened the knot of this tie and removed it. "Let's not waste a minute of it," she said as she unbuttoned his shirt, sliding her hands inside over his chest and pulling the shirt down over his arms.

Piece by piece, their clothing fell away until their bodies could touch the way they were meant to. . . .

Hours later, the two of them lay on the floor in front of the fire, a pillow under their heads and a blanket around them to keep them warm. Kendall, lying within the circle of Alexei's arms, kissed his shoulder.

He smiled and nuzzled his mouth against her hair. "You're awake."

"I'm afraid to fall asleep. We have so little time. I don't want to miss any of it."

Alexei pulled the blanket up around her a little more then rolled onto his side so he could look into her eyes. "I don't know how I'm going to let you go."

"You don't have to. I know that if I asked, I'd be allowed to stay."

"Oh, you'd be allowed to stay all right. But you'd never see your family again."

Kendall looked into his eyes. "You're my family now."

He pulled her body close to his and held her. "Oh, Kendall, I do love you. But you're going to be on that plane today, just the way you planned it."

They lay back on the pillow looking at each other, their faces only inches apart. Kendall traced a gentle finger along the corner of his mouth. "And then what?"

"I'll ask for permission to return to America."

"And what if they won't let you?"

"We'll worry about that when it happens."

Somewhere deep inside her, Kendall knew he wouldn't be allowed to come to her. "You could defect." She was grasping at straws and she knew it.

"Your country wouldn't allow it."

"Of course they would. People defect all of the time."

He shook his head. "Ballet dancers. Artists." He pushed her hair away from her face. "Our countries are going through a friendly phase right now and neither wants to do anything to disrupt that. If your country were to take me in without the permission of my country, it could destroy the delicate balance between them. Why would your country want to risk that when I bring them nothing?"

Kendall started to answer but he put a gentle finger over her mouth.

"The answer is that they wouldn't—unless they got something valuable in return."

"Do you mean information?"

"That's right. And I've admittedly had access to some sensitive documents." He kissed her on the forehead. "I want to be with you, but I won't turn traitor to my country to do it. I couldn't live with that kind of betrayal. Do you understand?"

Kendall nodded. "I would never ask it of you."

Alexei kissed her with a slow deliberation that left her trembling. Again they made love and for a short while slept in each other's arms.

And then it was time. They showered and dressed in silence. Alexei excused himself to make a phone call and while he was doing that, Kendall lovingly re-packed Anna's dress. Then she wandered around the cottage, gathering mental pictures to take home with her. She wanted to be able to imagine him here. She ran her fingers over the rich wood of his desk and the leather of his chair. Sitting down, she picked up some of his books. Poetry. History. The things he'd told her he was interested in.

She opened the book of poetry and found a white rose. Her white rose.

When Alexei walked into the room, she looked up at him. "You kept this?"

He kneeled beside her. "I thought it was all I'd ever have of you."

Tears suddenly sprang to her eyes as she threw her-self into his arms. "I don't want to leave you."

"I know." He stroked her hair and struggled to keep his own composure. "I don't want you to go." After a moment he held her away from him. "But you have to. Your plane is leaving soon." He stood up and held out his hand. "Come."

Kendall let him help her to her feet and into her coat. Alexei had arranged for a troika to meet them on the river. It was there and waiting. In silence the two of them journeyed to the city, and still in silence got into his car. Kendall looked at her watch. "I don't have time to go back to the hotel."

"What about your things?"

"Ginny was late once and I packed for her. I'll just have to hope she does the same for me."

Alexei put his car into gear and pulled into the light flow of traffic. Kendall stared out the window, twisting her gold wedding band, determined not to cry again.

Alexei watched her hands. He ached with the need to comfort her, but knew there was nothing he could do this time. "That ring," he finally said, "belonged to my mother. It's all I have left of my family."

Kendall gazed at the band's intricate design. "It's beautiful."

"My father was a goldsmith. He made it himself."

Kendall held out her hand and Alexei's closed securely around it, sending some of his strength into her.

The bus with Kendall's group on it had arrived at the airport just before them. Ginny was ushering everyone in, looking worried, when she spotted Kendall. Racing over to the car, she pulled open the door. "Where have you been? I was frantic!"

"I'm sorry. I probably should have called, but I was afraid someone might be listening in. Did you bring my things?"

"Yes. They've already been taken in." She reached into her purse and pulled out Kendall's plane ticket and passport. "I light-fingered this from the desk clerk at the hotel."

"Thanks, Ginny, I owe you."

Ginny looked past Kendall to Alexei and then back to Kendall. "You two certainly look glum."

"Ginny, would you mind going ahead without me? I'll catch up."

"We're boarding in a few minutes."

"I know. I'll be there."

Ginny straightened away from the car and closed the door. Kendall watched in silence as her friend walked into the airport, then turned to her husband. "I'm going to miss you so much." Her voice broke on the words.

Alexei pulled Kendall into his arms and just held her.

"Are you going to come in?"

"No." He stroked her hair. "I don't want to watch you leave."

She nodded against his shoulder. "I understand."

He held Kendall away from him and looked into her eyes. "I love you, and I'll find some way of getting in touch."

Kendall nodded. Her throat was tight with emotion.

Neither of them said goodbye when she got out of the car. It took all of her willpower not to turn around, but she knew if she did she'd go running back.

Ginny swooped at her from nowhere as soon as she entered the building, grabbing Kendall's hand and pulling her through the hallway. "Come on. They've already started boarding. These Soviets don't mess around.''

Kendall, dressed in the same jeans and sweater she'd been wearing the day before, showed the boarding agent her ticket and passport. He looked carefully at her and then examined her picture before finally waving her through. He did the same with Ginny. The two women walked across the tarmac together and boarded the plane.

Once they were on, Kendall and Ginny counted heads to make sure everyone had made it, then collapsed into their own seats.

"Now," Ginny said as she fastened her seat belt, "what happened last night? Where were you?"

Kendall lifted her left hand.

Ginny's mouth dropped open. "You married him?" she asked in something close to horror. "That's crazy. You're never going to see him again."

"Yes, I will."

"How do you know that?"

"Alexei will find a way."

"How? When?"

Kendall leaned her forehead against the window and stared outside. "I wish I knew. I really wish I knew."

Alexei drove about twenty miles out of the city to an area of country homes and parked in front of one that in America would have been considered a mansion. A woman in her late fifties answered the door and led him through the house to a library. A white-haired, jowly man sitting behind a massive desk looked up. "Alexei, come in. Close the door behind you."

He did, and sat in a chair across from the older man.

"I found your phone call this morning intriguing, to say the least." He leaned back in his chair and folded his hands over his round belly. "So, what is it that you want to talk to me about?"

Alexei looked the man directly in the eye. "I've fallen in love with an American woman, minister."

He didn't seem surprised. "And what are you planning on doing about it?"

In that moment, Alexei knew that the minister was already aware of exactly what he'd done about it.

"I've married her."

"I see."

"I'd like to be allowed to join her in America."

"Of course you would." The minister pursed his fleshy lips. Leaning forward, he pulled a file toward him, opened it and began reading. "This woman is named Kendall Stuart?"

"Yes."

"Daughter of Gen. Craig Stuart."

"Yes."

"An interesting choice of wife." The minister shook his head as he read the file, then set it aside and gave Alexei his full attention. "You realize, of course, that your request is denied out of hand. Your position has given you access to sensitive information."

"You have my word as a gentleman that the information will remain confidential."

"Your word?" He smiled. "I would be as much a fool as you to agree to that."

"I'm an honorable man."

For the first time the older man softened. "I know that, Alexei. But I have to explain my actions to others, and this I could never explain."

"I don't know what other guarantees I can give you. The fact that I want to join my wife in another country doesn't automatically make me a traitor to my own."

"Apparently not in your eyes. Your job with the government is over, of course."

The muscle in Alexei's jaw moved. He didn't give a damn about his job.

The minister looked at him with genuine regret. "I'm sorry, Alexei. There's nothing I can do. You're dismissed."

Alexei got wearily to his feet. There was no use arguing. He'd have to find another way.

As soon as the door closed behind Alexei, the minister picked up the phone.

Alexei controlled the helpless anger that welled within him as he left the dacha. For a long time he sat behind the wheel of his car thinking. He'd known this wasn't going to be easy. He'd find another way.

He was so absorbed in his thoughts that he didn't remember much of the drive to his apartment. As soon as he got out of his car, two men came walking toward him.

"Good afternoon," one of them said in Russian.

"What do you want, Breskov?"

"Oh, please, a little more respect. You and I are going to go for a drive."

"To where?"

"That hardly matters since you have no choice."

"I want an explanation."

"Very well. You, my friend, are being arrested."

Though he was surprised, Alexei's expression never altered. "And the charge?"

"You're a lawyer. You know I don't have to charge you with anything. I'm simply investigating your suspicious relationship with a certain American woman whose last name recently became Demyenov."

"Suspicious?"

"I think you've been passing secrets to her."

"You know that's not true. If it were you would have arrested her before she got on the plane to America."

"That would have made for a messy situation. Besides, I didn't want her. I wanted you."

"You're insane."

The agent smiled. "Perhaps. But I've got you right where I've wanted you for years, and there isn't a thing you can do about it." He signaled the other man with his hand and a moment later Alexei had a gun in his back. "As I was saying, nice day for a drive, isn't it?"

Chapter Ten

Kendall drove up to her mailbox and took out a handful of letters and magazines. She tossed the magazines onto the seat next to her and quickly went through the letters. Heartsick when she didn't find what she was looking for, Kendall placed them with the magazines. It had been three months since her marriage to Alexei and she hadn't heard a word from him. What could have happened?

She drove on to the stables and parked inside. As soon as she walked into the house, the dogs barked their friendly greeting. Absentmindedly, she gave them each a hug and a pat, then went to the living room and built a fire to take the chill out of the evening air.

Sitting in silence, she tried to figure out what to do. For weeks Kendall had wanted to go to the Soviet embassy to talk to somebody—anybody—about Alexei to see what they knew, but she was afraid she'd only make things worse for him.

The dogs growled suddenly and then ran barking to the front door. Kendall followed them and looked outside. A car was pulling up. Sergei Grinkov got out and began walking toward the house. She opened the door and waited, but he stopped halfway when he heard the dogs.

"Is it safe?"

"They won't harm you." She shushed the dogs and they immediately grew quiet.

He kept as wary an eye on the dogs as they kept on him as he walked onto the porch and into the house. Kendall led him into the living room and offered him a chair, but skipped the rest of the amenities in her anxiety over why he was there. "Have you heard something from Alexei?"

Sergei remained standing. "I've seen him."

Kendall wanted to be happy but there was something about the way Sergei was looking at her that told her his news wasn't good. "Where is he?"

His look softened at the tremor in her voice.

"They've locked him up."

"What?"

"He requested that he be allowed to leave the Soviet Union because of you and they've put him in some hideous asylum."

"My God," she breathed. "Why?"

"Because they want him to renounce you and admit that he passed you secret information. He refuses. They've caged him like an animal because he won't tell them what they want to hear."

The fingers on Kendall's right hand automatically went to her wedding band.

He pulled an envelope out of his pocket and handed it to Kendall. "Alexei asked me to give this to you. He also asked me not to tell you where he was, but I feel you have a right to know."

She held the letter to her heart as though it contained treasure. "There must be something we can do."

"If there is, I don't know what it could be. Now, if you'll excuse me, I must go before it's discovered that I came here."

"Of course. Thank you."

He inclined his head. "I can find my way out."

Kendall remained where she was in the middle of the room. She ran her finger lovingly over the outside of the envelope where Alexei had written her name. Closing her eyes for a moment, she opened the flap and removed the single sheet of paper.

My dearest wife
Sergei is here and has promised to deliver this letter to you. I've written to you every day that I could, but have been able to mail none of them. I imagine you've been worried about me. Please don't, darling, and know that I'm fine. Things here aren't going as well as I'd hoped. It may be a long while before we're together, but we will be together, Kendall. Never doubt that. I don't. Even during my most difficult moments. And never doubt that I love you. You give me life as surely as my heart beats. Don't despair.

Alexei

Kendall hugged the letter to her. She felt as though the life was slowly being choked out of her. What must he be going through?

Well, she wasn't going to sit here doing nothing any longer. Picking up the phone, she placed a call to her father's office. "Dad?" she said as soon as she heard his voice.

"Kendall! I'm glad you called. I thought I'd swing by your place tonight on my way home."

She didn't even hear him. "I have to talk to you."

There was a pause at the other end of the line. "It sounds serious."

"It is."

"Are you all right?"

"There's no way I can answer that, Dad."

Craig Stuart heard the urgency in his daughter's voice. "I'll be there in less than an hour."

In fact, he made it in under forty minutes and Kendall paced for each second of those forty minutes. As soon as she heard his car pull up she ran outside with the three dogs close behind her. Kendall threw herself into her father's arms.

He looked down into his only child's distressed face. "Baby, what's wrong?"

"Please come in, Dad. There's so much I have to tell you."

The two of them walked arm-in-arm into the house. Kendall settled her father into a chair then paced some more while she collected her thoughts.

Her father waited in silence.

Finally Kendall sat on the ottoman in front of him. "Dad, last year when you were in Europe and the Middle East on that special mission, I met a man. His name is Alexei Demyenov."

"I've heard of him."

"Well, actually, I did more than meet him. I fell in love with him."

Her father looked at her in silence.

"And when I was in Moscow on business I married him."

Her father's eyes narrowed. "You what?"

"Please don't be angry. I can't deal with that right now."

"Why are you telling me all of this, then?"

"We need your help. Because of me, Alexei's been put into an asylum." Her eyes sparkled with unshed tears. "Dad, they won't let him go until he renounces me and admits to being a spy. He won't do it."

The general took his daughter's cold, clenched hands between his thick, warm ones. "I'm sorry, honey. What can I do to help?"

"I've never before asked you to use your position to help me, but this is different. I don't know who else to turn to. I don't even know if you can do anything. I just know I can't bear the thought of Alexei being where he is and wondering what they're doing to him. Please, please, Dad, help me."

He squeezed her hands reassuringly. "I'll give it some thought and see what I can come up with."

"Thank you."

"Don't thank me yet. There are no guarantees."

"I know."

He rose to leave, but then looked at Kendall's pale face. "Are you going to be all right here alone? Would you like to come home with me?"

"I'd rather stay here. I'll be fine."

He pinched her chin between his thumb and forefinger. "Are you sure?"

"I'm sure. Thanks for the offer."

Kendall felt a small measure of relief as she watched him drive away. If anything could be done, her father would figure out what.

A day later, Kendall's office phone rang. It was her father. "Kendall, I want you to meet me at the Soviet embassy in exactly one hour. Don't ask any questions. Just be there."

He hung up before she could say anything.

Without telling Ginny where she was going and why, Kendall flew out of her office and arrived at the embassy half an hour early. They made her wait in the receptionist's office. When exactly one hour had passed from the time her father had called her, he strode in dressed in full military regalia, Colonel Tate by his side. He went straight to the receptionist. "I'm Gen. Craig Stuart and I have an appointment with Ambassador Brodsky."

She started to say something about sitting in the waiting area, but Kendall's father cut her off.

"Now. Is he available or not?"

Her eyes grew wide. "Yes, General. I'll tell him you're here."

A moment later the three of them were on their way to the ambassador's office.

The old man rose as they entered and shook hands, smiling kindly at Kendall. "Alexei's rose. It's nice to see you again. Please," he waved his hand, "be seated."

Kendall sat between her father and the colonel, wondering what was going on.

"Ambassador," her father said, "I'm a busy man and you're a busy man so I'll come right to the point. It seems that the U.S. government has something you badly want, and your government has something we want."

The ambassador inclined his head toward Kendall. "Should we be discussing this in front of your daughter?"

"No one in this room is more directly concerned than she is. I'd like her to stay."

"Very well. I bow to your wishes," said Brodsky.

"I've spent the past twenty-four hours on the telephone and have extracted an agreement from my government to a trade between our countries. You get the spy we caught last summer and we get Alexei Demyenov."

"The spy—if indeed he is such—is of no use to us. Why would we trade for him?"

"If I can be frank, Ambassador, we didn't have to offer the trade. We were simply trying to help your country save face."

The ambassador leaned back in his chair. "This is quite fascinating. And how, in your opinion, is this trade going to help us save face?"

"Because if you give us Alexei Demyenov, we won't publicize what you've done to him."

"Is that supposed to be some kind of threat?"

The general shook his head. "I don't threaten. I'm simply telling you the way it is. Your country has made a great effort over the past few years to airbrush its world image. Frankly, you've done a good job. But all of that hard-won confidence and goodwill you crave so much could be ruined if word of what you've done to Alexei were to get out. He's very well liked and respected, not just in America, but in all of the countries he's been in on the Soviet Union's behalf."

"What you say is true," the ambassador agreed.

"We can handle this situation in one of two ways. Either you make the trade with no one the wiser and come out a hero in the world's eyes for allowing Alexei to live in America with his wife, or you refuse and become the villain once again for keeping them apart."

"I see."

"Good. I'd hoped to make myself clear."

The ambassador looked at him curiously. "You're going to a lot of trouble on behalf of a man who has said that he won't discuss what he knows with the American government."

The general rose. "Every once in a while, Ambassador, we do something because it's right and not for what we can get out of it." He shook the older man's hand. "Good day. I'll expect to hear from either you or your representatives tomorrow."

"Tomorrow?" he asked, shocked. "I can't possibly have an answer for you by then."

"I suggest you cut through the—you'll pardon the expression—red tape and call me with a yes or no."

Kendall rose as well and looked curiously at the ambassador. "I thought you were Alexei's friend," she said quietly.

"I am. But he's had a fall from grace and I can't afford to be seen as sympathetic."

Colonel Tate, there apparently only as an observer, followed the general and his daughter out of the embassy. Kendall stood on the sidewalk and hugged her father. "Thank you."

"Thank me when you have your husband safely back."

"We both will. When do you think he'll be here?"

"If—and that's a big if, Kendall—they agree to the trade, the timing will have to remain confidential, even from you."

"I understand."

"And once he's free, there'll still be a time lapse between that and when you see him."

"As long as I know he's safe, I can wait for as long as it takes."

The weeks dragged by. Kendall's father hadn't mentioned anything to her and she hadn't asked. As she was sitting in her living room one evening reading, her father walked in.

She hadn't been expecting him. He was smiling. With her heart pounding, she stood up. "What?"

"Nothing. I just came by to say hello."

"Hello."

"And to deliver this." He handed her a large manila envelope. Kissing her cheek, he whistled as he walked out the door to his car. Kendall opened the envelope and looked inside. Almost reverently she lifted out the white rose and touched the soft petals to her cheek.

Alexei was safe.

Kendall opened the oven door and looked at her overdone tenderloin. "I don't know, Mom," she said to the petite blond woman who sat at the kitchen table. "If Dad doesn't get here pretty soon, his dinner's going to shrivel away to nothing."

"I'm sorry, Kendall. He's usually so punctual. I don't know what could be keeping him."

Kendall heard the front door open and suddenly the dogs, who'd been outside, all ran into the kitchen. Her father followed them in, leaned over, kissed his wife on the cheek and then smiled at Kendall. "Sorry I'm late but I think when you find out why you won't hold it against me."

There was a movement in the doorway behind him and Kendall suddenly found herself looking into Alexei's eyes. For a long moment she just stood there. Then she wordlessly crossed the room into his waiting arms.

Kendall's father touched his wife's arm and inclined his head toward the back door. Without saying anything, the two of them left.

Kendall looked up at Alexei and cupped his pale face in her soft hands. He'd aged ten years in the months since she'd last seen him. His face was tired and drawn. His dark hair had more gray in it. He'd lost a lot of weight. "Are you all right?" she asked softly.

Warm brown eyes gazed at her. "I am now."

"I got your rose a month ago. Where have you been all this time?"

"A hospital in Germany."

"A hospital? Why? What's wrong?"

"I had a few physical problems after I was released, but they're all taken care of now."

Kendall still looked worried.

Alexei smiled, and it was the same smile she remembered. "I'm all right now, really. Your father made sure of that."

"My father," she said, suddenly remembering her parents. But when she turned to introduce Alexei to her mother, she found them gone. She smiled and shook her head. "I guess they thought we needed to be alone."

"We do. I told your father I wanted to talk to you."

Kendall waited.

Alexei put his hands at her waist and lifted her onto the kitchen counter so that they were eye level. "Kendall, we've both been through a lot over these past months. I want you to know that if you've had second thoughts about our marriage, I'll understand."

"Second thoughts," she blankly echoed his words.

"It's okay."

Kendall shook her head as she gazed into his eyes. "Do you have any idea how much I love you? Being away from you all these months hasn't changed that."

"All of those wasted months," he said quietly. "We'll never get them back."

"We can't do anything about the past, but we still have our future."

Alexei smiled suddenly. "There speaks the optimist I know and love."

She touched his face again. "You look so tired."

"I am. I feel as though I could sleep for a week."

Kendall slid off the counter and took his hand in hers. "Come on. We can talk later."

While Alexei showered, Kendall turned down the bed and unpacked his only suitcase. There was very little in it and most of that was new. He'd had to leave everything behind.

When he came back into the bedroom, he had on drawstring pajama bottoms and no shirt, but there were bandages wrapped around his stomach.

Kendall looked at them but didn't ask any questions. He'd tell her when he was ready.

The sun hadn't quite gone down, so Kendall closed the blinds and drew the drapes while Alexei climbed into bed. She turned out the solitary lamp that was burning, took off her shoes and slipped into the bed next to him. His arm automatically came around her as she rested her cheek on his shoulder and draped her arm over his chest, careful not to touch the bandages.

"I'm so glad you're here," she said softly.

Alexei rubbed his mouth against her hair. "I was beginning to think it wouldn't happen."

Within minutes, Kendall heard his deep even breaths. He must have been exhausted. Carefully, so as not to wake him, she sat up and spent half the night just watching him sleep, afraid if she stopped he'd disappear and she'd find it was all a dream.

Just before dawn, Kendall couldn't keep her eyes open any longer. Curling her body around his, she fell asleep.

Suddenly the bed shook and Alexei yelled. Kendall, her heart pounding, sat up. Alexei was sitting up, too. Sweat beaded his forehead and his breathing was ragged.

"Alexei," she said softly. "Alexei. It's all right. You're home. You're with me."

His eyes slowly focused on her as he took a deep breath and exhaled. "I'm sorry."

"What's wrong?"

"Kendall, I . . ."

"Please, Alexei. Talk to me. What happened to you all those months?"

"Let's just say that I spent a lot of time being interrogated, and when the questioners didn't like the answers they were given, they let me know."

She gently touched the bandages on his stomach. "And this?"

"Broken ribs, but earned honestly in a fight with Breskov. He baited me while under the mistaken impression that I was manacled. And if it's any consolation, he looks worse than I do."

Kendall smiled, but it was tinged with sadness. "Look what I did to you."

Alexei shook his head. "No. It was my choice and I don't regret it."

"You've been banished from your homeland."

Alexei kissed the corner of her mouth. "For now. That might change in time. And if it doesn't, that's all right, too. What matters is that we're together. That's worth any sacrifice to me."

Putting his hands on her shoulders, he pressed Kendall quietly back against the pillows. Brown eyes gazed into gray. "I love you. It never ceases to amaze me how much. When I think how close I came to not even meeting you, I get a cold chill."

"We would have met somehow," she said.

"You sound so sure."

"Oh, I am." Her fingers outlined his mouth. "You're my fate and I'm yours. We had no choice but to meet."

"And no choice but to love."

Kendall crooked her finger at him. "Come closer."

He did.

"Closer."

He did again.

"Closer."

His mouth captured hers.

"That's better," she said softly, "but it's still not close enough."

"Have patience, darling. The best things take time. Trust me. It'll be worth the wait."

It was.

Epilogue

Three years later, Kendall quietly entered a classroom at Georgetown University and took a seat off to the side. Alexei spotted her and smiled. "Any questions?" he asked the class.

As he fielded a few of them, Kendall watched. He looked so much better now than he had when he first returned from the Soviet Union. He'd put the weight back on and was as strong as he'd ever been. His skin had regained its color. He still had nightmares, but they were growing less frequent.

As the students filed out, Kendall left her seat and walked over to him. "Is it all right to kiss the professor?"

Alexei pulled her into his arms. "Only if you're married to him."

As soon as their lips met, Kendall got that warm feeling in the pit of her stomach, just as she always did whenever he touched her.

Alexei smiled down at her. "What brings you here on your day off?"

"I just can't stay away from you."

"Besides the obvious."

Kendall grinned at him and stepped away so she could reach into her purse. She pulled out an envelope and handed it to him. "This came in the mail today. I thought you might like to see what it says."

He looked at the return address. "The results of my bar exam."

Kendall waited patiently.

Alexei started to open it, then stopped, then opened it. Looking at Kendall first, he drew the paper out and read it. The grooves in his cheeks deepened. "I passed."

"Of course."

He wrapped his arms casually around her waist, the letter dangling from his hand. "You know everything."

"You worked too hard to fail." She looked at him with gentle eyes. "Alexei, are you happy?"

He smiled at her. "What an odd question. Of course I am."

"Do you ever regret not being able to go home to Russia?"

"Yes," he said with quiet honesty. "Though regret is perhaps the wrong word. I'll never regret the choice I made to be with you. But there are times when I get a little homesick."

"I'm sorry."

"Don't be. All I have to do is look at you, and everything falls into place." He held up the letter again. "Remember what we said about starting a family once I had this?"

Kendall smiled. The answer was in her eyes.

"If you don't stop looking at me like that, we'll start it right here."

"Promises, promises."

*   *   *   *   *

Silhouette Special Edition®

NAVY BLUES
Debbie Macomber

Between the devil and the deep blue sea...

At Christmastime, Lieutenant Commander Steve Kyle finds his heart anchored by the past, so he vows to give his ex-wife wide berth. But Carol Kyle is quaffing milk and knitting tiny pastel blankets with a vengeance. She's determined to have a baby, and only one man will do as father-to-be—the only man she's ever loved...her own bullheaded ex-husband!

You met Steve and Carol in NAVY WIFE (Special Edition #494)—you'll cheer for them in NAVY BLUES (Special Edition #518). (And as a bonus for NAVY WIFE fans, newlyweds Rush and Lindy Callaghan reveal a surprise of their own....)

Each book stands alone—together they're Debbie Macomber's most delightful duo to date! Don't miss

**NAVY BLUES
Available in April,
only in *Silhouette Special Edition*.
Having the "blues" was never
so much fun!**

SE518-1A